PRA...

Eight Pieces of Eight
"...the Spanish colonial coinage, the 1724 shipwreck, **Tennessee caves**, and historical landmarks like the Henry Flagler Museum...evokes an atmospheric vibe of the age of Spanish exploration, while grounding the story in modern anxieties."—BookLife Publishers Weekly

Spanish Pieces of Eight
"In terms of writing, the real stars for me are the **British Virgin Islands** themselves. Lovingly and lavishly described, there's no doubt Rick Glaze has a real affection for these small gems of the Caribbean. Anyone who has been there will recognize them intimately. Anyone who hasn't will likely want to go."—Caribbean Compass Magazine

"...the diary-reading aspect does call to mind familiar tropes of classic pirate tales."—Kirkus Reviews

Ralph & Murray
"**Glaze is a skillfully** descriptive writer who effortlessly brings the world surrounding the animals to life..." —Kirkus Reviews, Starred Review

"**Glaze pens** fun, surprising scenes, blending small-town memories with the curious logic and big hearts of animals."—BookLife Publishers Weekly

"A funny, smartly observant, and philosophical animal tale; a **heartwarming read**."—Kirkus Reviews, Starred Review

PIECES OF EIGHT | BOOK 2

EIGHT PIECES OF EIGHT

RICK GLAZE

Also by Rick Glaze

Books

Ralph & Murray

Spanish Pieces of Eight

The Purple River

Jackass: Short Story Collection

Music CDs

Anegada Caribbean Breeze

Silicon Cowboy

Premium Reader Club

Join my Reader Club and be part of the excitement. I've enjoyed sailing and outdoor adventure for a long time and you can escape with me on these adventures by clicking below.

Get free books, free behind the scenes photos, original songs written for the books and more. Members are always first to hear about new offerings and publications. To join click on *Rick's Guide to the Virgin Islands* at:

https://www.RickGlaze.com

ScreenShot Publishers

Nashville, Tennessee

Ricksbooks@rickglaze.com

This book is a work of fiction. Names, characters, places, and incidents are the product of the author's imagination or are used fictitiously. Any resemblance to actual events, locales, facilities, or persons, living or dead, is coincidental.

Copyright ©2025 by Richard A. Glaze

ScreenShot Publishers First Edition

The scanning, uploading, and distribution of this book without permission is a theft of the author's intellectual property. Permission may be obtained by contacting Ricksbooks@RickGlaze.com.

Cover Design: Scott Simpson

Front Cover Painting: Acrylic/mixed media on canvas by Rick Glaze

Illustrations: Rick Glaze

Edit: Sam Severn

Proof Read: Ashley Hagan

ISBN Paperback: 979-8-9921937-1-8

ISBN Digital: 979-8-9921937-0-1

For
Betty Price

And For
Violet Saichek who might inherit her grandfather's itch someday

*Miracles are not contrary to nature, but only
contrary to what we know about nature.*

SAINT AUGUSTINE

PREFACE

With the adventure and intrigue of the Spanish Empire's dominance in the colonial period of history, I couldn't stop writing stories about the gold and silver coins lost to the shallow sands of the big blue ocean after only one book. The first in this series, *Spanish Pieces of Eight*, is the story of a Tennessee boy, Richard Dennison, discovering vast riches, a wide and deep ocean on which to hoist his sails, and mounds of pieces of eight. But it's the random opportunities and interactions with the people he meets, that tell his story. In the process of uncovering who he might be in life, he constructs a treasure hunt that launches his four children into their own self-discovery.

Bev Dahl, through a twist of fate, inherits the treasure-hunting gene from her grandfather to follow the scent of the coins. Unlike her grandfather however, Bev has help in her quest for clues while crawling through the vast and ancient limestone cave system in Tennessee. A powerful spirit Guru named Ezekiel is the wildcard for Bev, and for *Eight Pieces of Eight*.

PREFACE

Sure, the country music singer and part-time lawyer, Price Davis, and eccentric brother, Branson Dahl pitch in to upend cousin Mathias, and his diabolical obsession with the treasure. But as Ezekiel says, "This is Bev's adventure, not yours. You can turn the heat down for her, but she has to fight the fire."

My recommendation for you is to turn the page and get started.

CHARACTER LIST

Bev Dahl: Granddaughter of treasure hunter, Richard Dennison.

Alice Dennison Dahl: Mother of Bev.

Branson Dahl: Brother of Bev.

Mathias: First cousin of Richard Dennison and second cousin of Bev.

Walter Talon: Structural engineer.

Price Davis: Country music singer/lawyer, native of Nashville.

Andrew Dahl: Father of Bev.

Ezekiel: Spirit Guru.

Darien: Former boyfriend.

PROLOGUE

It was barely 7:15 when the morning sun broke on the eastern horizon and began filling Bev's bedroom with the light of a new day. Her mother always slept with no curtains or blinds on the windows so she would feel the full impact of the morning vibrations, saying it was her connection to the universe. Bev griped about it, and even made fun of her mother to friends about this practice that robbed a person of the last remnants of sleep.

Ironically, when she arrived at the condo in Palm Beach for this early Springtime getaway, she surprised even herself by following her mother's routine. The picture window displayed the full view of that golden ball hanging over the horizon as it slowly rose into the sky, illuminating the Atlantic Ocean and everything in its path. The roar of the surf breaking on the white sand beach burst into the room as Bev inched the sliding glass door open. Her lungs filled with the salty ocean air as she inhaled a deep breath.

I am not mimicking my mother, she thought to herself. *I just like the morning sun...for this trip...only...it won't last...it's not forever, I know I'll make the bedroom dark again, it's not forever.*

"I am not my mother!" She yelled at the bathroom mirror, staring with amazement at her reflection, but the mirror didn't respond. She stuck her tongue out at the mirror and grimaced with her worst face. Finally after a prolonged silence, the reflection replied, *Okay, you are not your mother, just get over it.*

Bev started to reach for her phone to participate in the daily ritual of flooding her mind with irrelevant, useless dribble that thousands of people worked all night to deliver to a simple handheld device that looks innocent but was the vehicle for self-debasement and destruction, but she consciously diverted herself to a fresh grapefruit instead. The second time she reached for the phone, her hand never made it, but diverted to the ring attached to the door key, and her feet followed the leader, taking her through the front door, down the elevator to the lobby where her copy of the Miami Herald was folded and waiting. Her paper cup filled with lobby-coffee and with the newspaper under her arm, she rode the elevator back to the 12th floor. Dropping the key on the table, she headed to the east facing deck, coffee and paper in hand. Bev flopped down in the reclining chair and gently opened the paper to the front page and went into shock.

CRYPTO COLLAPSES LEAVING HAPLESS INVESTORS FLAT

"Crypto's rocket ship to Mars, collapsed back to earth in a fiery crash in trading yesterday," she read. "Bitcoin is the popular way to describe this currency, but that is a misnomer implying there is some kind of 'coin', but there is no coin. It is merely a blockchain or series of complex transactions. No assets or collateral underlie this new-age currency. It's cyber-equations, and this equation equals zero. Spring break is over for the crypto crowd and blood is in the streets."

Bev let the newspaper slip to her lap. Her hand started to reach for the coffee cup, but instead slammed against the paper. *What about the bank and the 19 percent interest*, she thought.

Terror engulfed her like a wave. *Mine is a stablecoin tied to other currencies. For god's sake it's a crypto bank.*

She picked the paper back up, "Many people were attracted to the high rate of return and promised stability while heaving a combined $50 billion into it. Over the first few days of the month, stablecoin lost its peg currency and both currencies plunged to near zero. There is no liquidity and all investor assets are worthless."

Bev broke into a cold sweat while the iconic view of the Atlantic in front of her faded, behind a shroud of confusion. She was simultaneously furious at her boyfriend Darien, who got her into this, incredulous at Wall Street, disheartened with government, angry at the Miami Herald, terrified of the future, and embarrassed at her naivety and stupidity, to bet a million dollars on this dumb thing, but most of all what would she tell her mother?

Humility rolled in like a black cloud filling every corner of her being. She was the person, like famous treasure-hunting icon, Grandpa Richard, who feared nothing, who measured only the risk of losing opportunity, not weighing the risk of failure. But now her wings melted in the hot sun and she fell to the hard, cold ground. Her brother, Branson and her dad...both losers, fantasy purveyors, leaders of their own strange pack, no rudder, no clue, eccentric, fell into wealth, born on third base and think they hit a triple. But not her. She was smarter, more savvy, more "in touch" with her world!

I've got to call Mom...I can't call Mom.

Bev's eyes did not focus and she barely made it to the bedroom. Pulling the curtains turned the room dark and she crawled in bed pulling the covers over her head to begin the process of soaking the sheets with cold sweat.

CHAPTER
ONE

When Walter Talon gave the map to Mathias with no expectations, he did have a big dose of curiosity about what Mathias would do with it. Walter himself pored over the map for several years and even followed his instincts and his best guess to what this treasure was and more importantly, where it was. He faintly recognized some landmarks, and researching them led him to locations in Alabama, Georgia, and Florida, and later a faint indication into Tennessee.

Some of the places turned out to be dead-ends with no hint of the treasure, but the Tennessee location looked promising, if even illogical. It was out of context with the origin of this Spanish lost treasure. Walter tracked down these coins to a massive wreck off the south Florida coast in the summer of 1724. The massive wooden ship broke up on the coastline and dumped its cargo in the shallow ocean sand near the Marquesas Keys, a few miles from Key West. The vessel broke up in pieces which resulted in the loot being scattered like grains of sand for miles. Walter's research uncovered that the assayer was Jose Eustaquio at the mint in Mexico from the letter "J" on the shield side of the coin. The obverse side, showing the coat-of-arms, displayed reigning monarch, King Phillip V.

The wreck was famous at the time and much of the cargo was recovered by the relentless and over-bearing Spanish government. It was a fearful time because getting exposed pocketing even one silver piece of eight resulted in unceremonious public hanging. Ships logs reveal about 120 tons of gold and silver coins sunk to the bottom along with over 500 sailors, nobility, and clergy lost. According to reports, 80 percent of the precious treasure was recovered over the next ten years, but with that much metal, raw opportunity, and bribery, no doubt some of it found its way elsewhere.

Walter was giving up on the treasure at his age after admitting to himself that he obsessed about the details constantly for years. He had a handful of silver pieces of eight, and less than a half dozen gold doubloons for his effort, but the quest had bested him and he eagerly passed it on to Mathias, not bothering to guess whether it was a gift or a curse.

The day Walter nonchalantly offered the map to Mathias, he also thrust on him a box with miscellaneous contents he collected during his search. Walter did get clues during his time studying the map. One led him to northern Alabama. He couldn't be sure, but when he arrived there, the map seemed to be pulling him in a south-east direction and all the way to a partially hidden cave entrance, grown over with no sign of footprints, or human traffic.

He had no intention of going deep into that cave, but as strange as it seemed, the map was beckoning him into the cold, moist and muddy darkness. He followed the call, even crawling on his belly in the wet clay. When the passageway opened to a cavern at least forty feet high, he flashed his light around the walls, finally catching a slight glint in the far corner. The first thing he saw was a hole in the ground about four-feet wide and a few feet deep. It didn't look like a fresh dig, but it didn't have the trappings of a long period of water erosion. Clearly something had been removed.

On his knees, he sifted around the surrounding soil, first finding a dirt-caked round object. He scraped off some mud with the front of the flashlight then pulled the light back to illuminate it. That was his first glimpse of a Spanish Piece of Eight. After finding a few more, his light found the glow of shiny gold and a two-dollar gold coin. His first doubloon.

Walter made note of the way in and out of the cave and returned many times to look for more clues, but nothing materialized. On one of his last visits, he looked at the map and noticed that the directions that got him to the cave had faded away. He was sure that he could never find it from the map any longer.

It was hard for him to admit that the map was changing, rationalizing that it was old and merely fading. That was a good explanation...but Walter never quite believed it. He took one last look at the map, nodding with resolve that the directions to his cave were completely missing with no reference to even the landmarks that led him there. Instead, the lines and landmarks appeared to point north, up through Alabama and into Tennessee. Something else was going on here. Something that intrigued him, while at the same time scared the pants off him.

CHAPTER
TWO

Mathias filled his mug for a third time with black coffee and sat at the kitchen table. He reached into his pocket; his fingers wrapped around a familiar, round coin, touching it like a blind man reading braille. His memory transported him out of Tennessee, to Palm Beach and the past events that changed everything.

Standard Oil Barron Henry Flagler built Whitehall Mansion as his winter home in Palm Beach. After his death, it was a hotel for a period, and in 1963 was restored and became the Flagler Museum.

Mathias had been on an engineering team cleaning up a mess around the canal on the west side of the museum. When they ran into a big problem, the managers called in a supervisor from the original team that had torn down the ten-story hotel addition, in order to restore it to the original footprint, from sixty years earlier.

Walter Talon strolled onto the construction site, and walked up to Mathias on a mud bank near the west side of the building. He stopped looked down, kicked a clump of dirt and carefully watched it roll down the bank into the canal.

"I hear you guys need a little help on this standing water," Walter said facing Mathias but looking at the canal.

Mathias knew who he was without any introduction. Walter Talon was twenty years his senior, and had a reputation in south Florida for being tough, ornery, colorful, and always right on tricky questions in the construction business.

"Drain is in, and it looks good. Pumps are working, but she's still floodin' out." Mathias said.

"Look son, when they built that ten-story add-on, they never finished out the drain system the right way. Once they got the steel in they couldn't go back," he continued. "Two of the rooms facing west down there in the basement flooded regularly. That's just the way it was."

"Okay, I get it but I've got to fix it. What do we do?" Mathias answered.

"Start with a retaining wall on the canal, then dig out all that mud and replace it with that new silica compound. It's a bigger job than it looks," he said.

Walter was splitting his time between his house at Lake Worth, near Palm Beach, and his family home in Valdosta, Georgia. Like everybody, his close ties and friendships in the construction business in Florida slowly faded as retirement sunk in, and he was spending more time as a gentleman farmer, in Valdosta, just over the state line in what some liked to call North Florida. That was because the flat landscape, sand, and beach feel of Florida did not stop at the state line.

Mathias took a breath and looked up from his recollections, stroked the coin in his pocket, and sat back in his chair, to let his mind reach back again to the past.

He thought about when he pulled onto the long driveway in Valdosta for the first time, past corn fields, and pastures and up to the two-story frame house that was still in Walter's family after 200 years.

He saw a rider darting across the pasture, toward the house, in a brisk cantor on a jet-black quarter-horse. He recognized Walter from a few hundred yards out, sitting on a western saddle under a white straw Wrangler hat. Mathias was stopping in on his drive from Florida to his hometown just south of Nashville. He made the trip regularly, and over time made stopping at the farm a standard part of the journey.

One evening after dinner and a little scotch tasting, Walter opened his palm to show Mathias a gold coin about the size of a silver dollar. Even in low light, the coin glistened with a rich luster. He handed it to Mathias.

"It's a Spanish doubloon minted in Mexico in 1724," he said.

"Doubloon? What does doubloon mean?" Mathias asked.

"It's a two-dollar gold piece. The Spanish minted them for 350 years during what people call the colonial period. You know, colonies and all that," Walter had said.

Mathias pulled his thoughts back again from those past years, to present time, in his kitchen in Tennessee as he lifted his cup for another sip. He took a long, deep breath, and looked out the window. In his mind's eye he saw his hand reaching out to give the coin back that night years ago, but Walter's hand gave a slight pushing motion in the air and said, "It's for you. Keep it."

It all started there, and later the map, and the digging and searching. It never ended and now the map is talking to him; what would be next? He wanted desperately to give up this insane treasure hunt, but somehow he never could do it. And now... now he was drawn to the treasure more than ever. It was a clamp on his mind that compelled him to care about it more than anything else.

Mathias let his recollections fade away as he glanced at the weekly community newspaper lying on the table. Then his eyes moved to the handwritten list of Christmas cards to his family and friends. In the past he had created maps to nowhere and to nothing, simply decoration and amusement for his annual card. He modeled them after decorative pirate maps from books he'd borrowed from the library. When he bumped into friends in his little two-street downtown, they'd ask things like, where does that map go? Did an elf give you that map? One cousin asked, is that where the end of the rainbow is?

He was obsessed with maps, but he never tipped his hand that he was onto a grand treasure hunt, a treasure that would dwarf the resources of anybody in his town and heck, maybe everybody combined in that town.

This year's map was different from all the previous ones. Before he produced the card, he pored over the real treasure map, and started seeing small spots light up in short pulses. A pencil mark on these spots, plotting and measuring to make any sense of these locations, rendered no explanation or insight, until one day a low but distinct voice echoed through his ear, "She will come, show her the map."

Surprised and a bit dumbfounded, he sat in front of the map for days making new pencil marks, turning it sideways, shining incandescent, then infrared light on it. He took it outside and shook it; everything he could think of, until back inside in the low light of a cloudy early-evening dusk, the voice finally spoke to him again.

"She will find the treasure or you will die trying."

He sat still staring out the window, un-nerved, and shaken. *What in god's name is this voice about*, he thought. *Who is talking to me?*

Mathias racked his brain with thoughts about how to proceed from here. He had been close to the treasure. He knew it deep down in his soul. So close. He had found a few gold doubloons and silver pieces of eight, all with the same mint date, 1724, scattered on the cave floor. He could smell the distant aroma of victory, but could not put his hands on the big cache of coins and the real prize. He trusted no one and shared his quest with no one.

Who could this "she" be? How do I find her? And most important, if she finds it, how do I get it away from her?

"It's mine. All mine," he thought. "I'm not sharing a single coin."

He walked to the bathroom, stared into the mirror, stood back on his heels and repeated, "I'm not sharing a single coin. All mine. Yes, all mine," He watched the reflection of himself nodding in agreement. He was resolved.

This year's Christmas card was a direct copy of the original, scaled back to fit a conventional envelope. In his mind's eye, he pictured the foldout map and gold leaf cover of the card. This is the biggest chance he had ever taken. He was virtually showing the real map to the world, the map to "his" treasure.

It was a Hail Mary attempt to find out who the "she" was that the voice in his ear was talking about. In his desperate attempt to identify the person who could find the treasure, he was risking it all. As he made his way to the post office to mail the cards, he was very tense and on high-alert. Every car door that slammed, or sudden flash of light caused him to flinch. Normal things felt amplified while the non-normal things, like sirens, were over-the-top fear-provoking.

He would wait and be ready for whatever came next.

CHAPTER
THREE

Last Christmas and only a few months before her trip to Palm Beach, Bev headed home to California for the holiday break. She was on an investment banking team in New York, and had only one deal closing by year-end. The lawyers had the details covered, so she was off the hook and out of the office for two weeks. Her normal route home was non-stop to San Jose, but the flight got scrubbed and they put her on a plane to the nearby airport in San Francisco.

Nobody liked driving to San Francisco airport, but her dad, Andrew, made the trip to SFO from the Santa Cruz mountains up I-280, the major artery connecting Silicon Valley to San Francisco. It was six in the evening and the commute traffic was snaking its way up past the San Andreas fault line where the coastal fog had burned off hours before, giving Andrew the usual tree-covered view of the low mountain range separating the Valley from the Pacific Ocean.

Bev jumped in the car with a big grin, hugged her dad, and uttered his favorite warn-out saying, "Let's bolt this pop-stand." For a split second before he pressed the gas pedal, Andrew regarded Bev's Wall Street look. Her shoulder-length black hair was now cropped above her ears and parted neatly on the right side, every hair in place. Andrew nodded imperceptibly and thought, *the business look.*

As the car inched its way off the curb and into the slow-flow of traffic, they maneuvered north a half mile, and then made their way onto the south-bound highway.

Like all kids arriving home with their minds full of their new city and new job, halfway wanting to blab about all they've seen and learned, and the other half trying on the adult role of being "cool" with it all. A "what's the big deal" attitude. Bev covered new ground and said, "Dad, what's new with you?"

Bev expected that her dad was still in the throes of fantasy deal-making, as in buying islands, becoming a big publisher of poetry books, scraping hillsides for new luxury neighborhoods, and on and on. She wasn't disappointed.

The "old Dad," from growing up who was laid-back, easy-going, make-things-right-with-the-world, started to fade away after he succeeded uncovering the clues to the nearly impossible treasure hunt that her Grandpa Richard had left the family. Bev's mom and dad got their share of the gold and silver coin bonanza, but Andrew ultimately saw only a small portion of the loot, because Alice couldn't be married to the "new" Andrew. She built him a bungalow at the edge of her ranch with a view of the Pacific Ocean, gave him five million dollars in silver pieces of eight, and unceremoniously divorced him.

Andrew was a poet in his 20s, when he met Alice in college at Berkeley, and seamlessly settled into his chosen career path of writing poetry, by saying a simple "I do," and marrying the "rich girl." But the saying that money changes everything hit home like a bullet, shot from a gun. The side of Andrew that was well hidden and virtually unknown to anybody came oozing out when these vast sums of silver and gold surfaced.

Andrew reveled in the opportunity to converse with his

daughter, so he plowed right in, "My new publishing company is getting off the ground, and I'm really excited, because I got a grant to launch it. It's not about the money so much, but more about the Arts Council in the city buying into my plan."

Bev shuffled in her seat, "Cool Dad."

"It's about bringing underserved voices into the world… there's a great need," he continued.

Bev looked out the window to a cloud covered sun setting over the coastal hills and rolled her eyes, "All right, Dad. Good work."

In a half-hearted stab at flipping the conversation she said, "What's my little brother, Branson up to?"

"He's got a couple of new projects, and he's learning to fly helicopters with me," he replied. "We're close to getting licensed in an Airbus H Series. It's not a long distance bird and it only has room for five passengers, but you can land it anywhere."

"Did you buy a helicopter, Dad?" She said.

"Not yet. Still deciding what model I need."

Bev was relieved to see her mother's house right then, as they pulled into the driveway. She jumped out and ran to the front door. Andrew carried her two soft bags to the front porch, nodded when Alice came to the door and then sped off down the road.

Christmas was a week away but decorations were up and ready for a merry, white Christmas, even as the forecast was for mid-70s and sunny. Bev sank into a big chair with a cup of tea, took a deep breath and let her mind think of nothing. Alice let her daughter unwind bowing to her sense that catching up on Bev's life, and all that is New York, would be revealed in its own sweet time.

After a while, Bev pried herself out of the chair on the sun-filled porch, and headed back to the kitchen for a tea refresh.

She strolled quietly through the house, her long legs fanned by the wispy calico skirt she snitched from her mother's closet. Walking by the fireplace, she saw a cluster of greeting cards on the mantel. One struck her as odd and a bit out of place. Picking it up by its gold leaf cover, she began to open it and then opened it more and then opened more until she was staring at a map, but not a road map, or geography map, but more like a pirate map with faint illustrations and strange symbols. She tried to make sense of it by looking for some context of north/south, or familiar places, but she didn't recognize anything.

"Hey Mom, what's this big Christmas card that's a map or something?" she said as she stepped into the kitchen.

"Oh that one. That's from cousin Mathias. You've seen those before; he sends some crazy map thing every year," Alice said

"I don't remember those," Bev replied.

"Mathias is Grandpa Richard's first cousin from down in the south. All Grandpa's relatives are in the south, most in Tennessee," Alice said.

"Did I meet him when I was little?" Bev asked.

"Oh yes, he was always around, and maybe closer to my age than Grandpa's.

Seemed pretty much normal then, but he's gone a bit eccentric with these treasure map things," Alice replied.

Bev walked across the kitchen to the tea pot, filled her cup and then added honey and squeezed in a wedge of lemon.

"Do you see kind of a funny light reflection or something on this map, Mom?"

"Nope, nothing like that," Alice replied.

Bev walked back to her chair, stopping to replace the card on the mantel, but instead tucked it under her arm and took it with her to her chair on the porch. A sip of tea, then she began to open the map again. With it fully spread out on her lap, she noticed one of the lines was starting to glow ever so slightly.

She put her finger on the spot and moved it along the glowing line. Then she pulled her finger from the surface and as she did the glow receded and disappeared.

"Mom?" she yelled. "Mom you've got to see this."

Meanwhile Christmas came and went and weeks had gone by since Mathias mailed the cards. Nothing had happened. No calls, no visitors, no letters in the mail, not even an email… radio silence. He looked at the list. There was no rhyme or reason why anybody on his stodgy old Christmas list would have a connection to this map much less the treasure.

He thought to himself in the silence, *okay so, you're hearing voices. Other people hear voices. The evangelists hear voices. The prophets heard voices. I know other people hear voices; I get it. But hey man, you're not a whack-job like those kinds of people!*

He picked up the list and took a quick look, turned it over and slammed it face down on the table. *And now my map is floating around in the world. What was I thinking?*

He slammed his fist against the table and wallowed in the silence. *Nobody will know what they are looking at*, he thought.

He grabbed the small water glass from the table, walked over to the kitchen counter snagging a cube of ice and turned up the bottle of Jack Daniels for a healthy splash of whiskey. Sipping from the glass he sat down, turned the list back over and punched in the phone number of the first name on the list.

"Jackson, are you hiding, where you been?" He spoke into the phone.

"Hell man, we ain't farming today, it's too cold. Just knocking around in the barn most days. I'm trying to make that tractor last another year. Still got to feed those cows every day. You know, always a little something," he said.

"How was your Christmas?" Mathias said.

There was a brief silence and although not expecting it, he knew why. That was a lady's comment for small talk. 'How was Christmas', goes along with 'I'll bet your Christmas table looked beautiful', and 'did Melissa make it home this year from Chicago?' Guy talk was, 'did that old mare of yours make it through the cold spell.'

But Mathias didn't give a rats-hind-end about that old mare. He was probing for any comment about the map.

He called one at a time working his way down the list and at the halfway mark, nobody mentioned the map. His card was probably buried at the bottom of everybody's Christmas stack... lost and forgotten.

He rolled a doubloon around between his fingers, unfurled the map and then looked up and said out loud, "I'm going back to the cave. I still think the big stash is there...somewhere in that cave...it's got to be."

CHAPTER
FOUR

Mathias sprayed a light stream of water on the shiny surface of his maroon Ford F-150. Then he stepped off the driveway and scooped up a handful of dusty soil, flung it at the truck, and watched the dust adhere to the tiny beads of water. Another scoop or two did the trick and Mathias was ready to drive to the caves in the morning. His truck was new and well kept, but he needed to make sure it looked like a working vehicle from out in the country. No special attention...just a regular, ole truck.

The caves were down an isolated country road paved in nothing but dirt and tall weeds, but that's precisely why any unusual movement was noted and would look suspicious. These limestone caves are part of a vast ancient network extending from Kentucky through Tennessee and into Alabama. But this is local country, and country people watch out for intrusions and trouble; a culture deeply rooted in religion and the rural-unspoken cult of "I've got your back."

Mathias planned to leave around dawn the next morning with an arrival at the caves as early as possible. He climbed the stairs to his storage area in the attic, flipped on the light and saw the box just as he left it. The box he inherited from Walter was a milk crate with rope-handles attached by small brass screws; a few painted-on red letters partially rubbed away obscuring the original words.

Sitting down on a hardware-store plastic stool, he peered over his shoulder with a subconscious, paranoid gaze to make sure he was alone. Sifting through the box, he looked for the doubloons first, and then the pieces of eight. Satisfied they were both there, he reached for the trowel and hammer that Walter included with the small bit of paraphernalia. Mathias always used these relics of his predecessor's exploration for no good reason other than a made-up superstition that he imagined would help his search. Although when Walter handed the box along with the map to Mathias, he gave him no background or mention of his own attempts at solving the mystery.

Mathias laid the tools beside the box and reached for the folded parchment at the bottom. He had noticed it, but had never given it much thought in the past. Tonight for some unknown reason, he laid it unopened next to the digging tools that were going with him to the caves.

As the morning sun rose breaking through the roofs of the out buildings surrounding the house, Mathias steered the dirty-looking Ford truck onto the two-lane country road and pointed it into the rising sun. He glanced down to the passenger seat to confirm the map was riding comfortably next to him. The engine purred softly and the still of the morning featured bird songs and calls back and forth from the fields as he patiently drove.

After turning off Highway 70, he saw the familiar sign, "Hay for Sale," nailed to the light pole and took the next left onto the dirt road for the twenty-minute ride to the cave. A wide left curve in the road slowed him down a bit, but just as the turn tightened, a bobcat darted into the road in front of the truck. Mathias slammed on the brake just as he felt a thump. Putting the truck into park, he opened the door and walked around to see what damage there was. Laying just under the front bumper was a half-stunned animal who seeing Mathias, could only lay there, his body not responding to the fear in his eyes. Mathias knew if the animal were merely stunned, he'd get up and head for the field eventually. If bleeding internally, it'd most likely be a goner.

He walked back around and climbed into the cab. Everything on the seat was on the floor of the cab. He bent over and picked up the parchment first and turned it over in his hands. Starting to toss it on the seat, he stopped and, without thinking, unfolded it until he could see the drawing. The angle he was holding it, caused him look closer and for the first time recognized the shape of the drawings. It was a primitive rendition of the all-important treasure map.

Quickly grabbing both maps, he laid this new find over the other, seeing the scale was not the same, but it was the same big picture. Mathias's forehead broke into a sweat, and anxiety riveted him from head to toe. *Had he missed something...an important piece of the puzzle. Another detail slowing him down. Walter never mentioned it. How would I have known. What does Walter know that he's not telling?*

He looked up and his eyes focused deep into the scruffy, unkept field. He could smell the morning dew evaporating off the wild grasses lining the road. Then looking down, he saw it. The right side of each map was different. The simple rendition, pointed south, while the big map turned north. After reorienting it north/south, what he saw could not be happening.

He sat back on the road, let the maps go and with both hands rubbed his eyes. He looked at the maps again.

The big map changed in front of Mathias, while he was looking at it, while the simple rendition remained the same. *This cannot be...what have I got myself into?* The left side, at the beginning, was fading away and the target direction was moving east. East that is, away from this cave that he was driving to; this cave that he pinned all his hopes on. *This is a fool's errand, a time killer...no, a time bomb.* He sighed. *This treasure hunt is a soul-less assassin.*

When Mathias reached the cave, he dragged himself to the entrance while muttering, *I'm done...I'm really done...no more.* He pulled the broken limbs and rocks away from the narrow entrance, and flipped on his monster flashlight. Turning for one last look over his shoulder, he saw no one and no movement and he felt it was safe. Then he walked through the entrance into the dark and out of the light.

After about 200 feet, he took a deep breath, and exhaled to jam himself through the narrow passageway between the limestone walls that he called "fat-man squeeze." A low duck-walk was next before he could stand up in the damp cavern. He shined the light at his feet, took a slow walk around, and stopped at the four-foot-wide crevice he had just come through. Taking a deep breath he shouted, "that's it; I am SO done with this...this stupid treasure hunt."

CHAPTER
FIVE

Back in Palm Beach, just before noon, the phone rang. Bev rolled over after the fifth ring and looked at the display. Darien was calling from his office. She pointed a finger toward the button, but instead let the ringing trail off to silence. Her arm collapsed back onto the sheet. She was still holding the phone when it dinged letting her know Darien sent her a voicemail. Pulling the pillow over her head and rolling back over, she ignored the phone and the message...not ready to talk to anyone and especially Darien.

The investment of $300,000 was lost! But, every pore in her body oozed cold sweat as she recanted the hard facts. Using her investment as collateral, she had borrowed more than twice that to buy this crap. Not much math required... she lost a million dollars.

The early afternoon inched by while Bev watched the slivers of light peeking through the curtains from her bed. She ignored her mother's calls. The brokerage house called. She ignored it. She knew what they wanted. Her collateral had disappeared and they needed money.

The touches of sunlight squeaking through started to fade

as the daylight waned, and Bev coaxed one leg out from under the covers and onto the floor. She sat up, ran her fingers through her hair and inched into the bathroom. Flipping on the light, she stared at a head of jet-black hair in a boyish, but strikingly Wall Street style. Dark eyebrows hung above faded mascara, over dark circles, a touch of red still clinging to her lips. She broke out crying, barely getting her hands to her face in time to catch the torrent of tears. Her back collapsed against the wall as her knees gave in to the slow pull of gravity, and she slumped onto the floor.

CHAPTER
SIX

Walter Talon didn't exactly hold back his knowledge of the map, coins, and his own quest. He merely handed the map and box over to Mathias, confused and not really believing himself, that any of this had substance or might be worth pursuing. But he was not convinced that it should be thrown out and ignored. *Mathias is a big-boy*, he rationalized. *Let him decide.*

Walter felt light hearted, like a weight was off his back, after he was rid of the map. But he continued to see a picture in his mind's eye of the map changing directions...going north toward Tennessee where Mathias lived among generations of his own family.

Walter grew up a country-boy in a farming community. He went to school with his neighbors and was a proud member of the Future Farmers of America. He learned the best way to raise cattle and when to plant corn and soybeans...and how to manage the financials of a farm. But Walter was singled out early on by a teacher named Mrs. Smyth. She discussed with his parents the sense of Gestalt, or big picture view he possessed.

Not only that, his math scores were at the top of the chart. His parents were good people, but tied to the land from birth.

They agreed to go along with emphasizing math in school and the unusual move of special tutoring to make sure he was prepared and competitive. He applied to engineering schools in Alabama and Florida, but in the end took a full scholarship to Georgia Tech in Atlanta. His first job was in construction in Florida.

IN HIS QUEST for clues about the map, he had looked around the internet. He was astounded to discover that a giant limestone cave system stretched from Kentucky through Middle Tennessee and into northern Alabama. It is the most extensive limestone cave system in the world. Cave art, carbon-dated back 4,000 years, has been found, and more than seven thousand deep caves are recorded in Tennessee alone.

He came across an arial map of the largest concentration of known caves. What he saw amazed him. On one search, he viewed a three-dimensional map of a broad area in Tennessee most known for the underground caves. This cutting-edge technology displayed images of sinkholes and cave entrances clearly, in the middle of dense forests...places that would never be identified unless you were standing next to them. But in the end, none of it persuaded him to keep trying.

Walter was a sociable kind of guy with a monthly golf game, a poker group, and he could hang pretty well at the local diner. He had nearly busted at the seams to tell these bored retirees about this crazy adventure, but every time he opened his mouth to spout-out the latest phenomenon, no words would come. It was like his mind turned blank. So, Walter never mentioned the map, the hunt, or the coins...or the caves. Nothing. It was all his to know, and now it all belonged to Mathias.

PIECES OF EIGHT

CHAPTER
SEVEN

The orange sun laid low in the western sky when Bev flipped the secured latch pushing open the wooden gate that led to the beach. Her bare feet strolled somberly through the dry, puffy sand for about fifty yards until the sand firmed up, wet from the receding tide. She looked north toward the town of Palm Beach, then turned to look over her right shoulder south to Miami. The ocean waves were pounding the beach, but had left an apron of wet sand as it careened toward a low tide. The setting sun dribbled into her eyes as she shuffled down the beach, Miami bound.

Bev forced herself to think of her peaceful childhood, almost a California fairy tale. A ranch on top of the Santa Cruz mountains with sparse but poignant views of the Pacific Ocean. A dad always around; a nurturing mother with lots of kid activities; a grandmother and above all Grandpa Richard. Money was never a topic or a concern or a restricting element. Summers were cool and even on the hot days, a sweater was useful at night. She remembered one winter the pond near the house froze over with a thin sheet of ice and she could toss a rock and watch it slide to the center, but that was only one time. Sure, they had jackets, 'cause the moist winter air felt cold, but it wasn't the deep freeze of Lake Tahoe, or Boston or those places. She chuckled thinking of Mark Twain's saying, *the coldest winter he ever spent was summer in San Francisco.* She could rate the weather in that city, forty minutes north, as fair, but not pleasant. It was always too cold for her.

Jennifer, her grandmother, led trips to the Virgin Islands, most of the time staying on the little round island near the airport, Marina Cay in the British Virgins. She could hear Grandma saying, it reads like 'day' but sounds like 'bee.' Meaning 'Cay' was pronounced like 'Key'. She and Branson would run around the island repeating that phrase to all who would listen. *Reads like day but sounds like bee.* Then they'd make their arms into wings and fly around like buzzing bees.

The two of them made a fort in the Rob White house, the concrete building on top of the island. Her mother set up a makeshift playhouse in the basement and when they had friends visit, they'd put on plays. Grandma always wanted more plays and laughed through all of them. But Bev remembered the goosebumps running up her back in that cold basement, too afraid Branson would tease her if she complained.

Bev looked down the beach at the line of high-rise condos and the smattering of fellow beachcombers, and let her mind wonder back to things like freshman year at Stanford. A jogger swished past her in the wet sand on the ocean side; a thin guy wearing a swim suite, and no shirt. Mildly brown skin like a middle easterner, he ran with a steady even gait. Just ahead she saw him maneuver around patches of newly deposited seaweed. Sidestepping that gooey mess, Bev looked down to see the fresh footprints of the jogger. The hard edge of the imprint in the wet sand was quickly crumbling when without thinking, Bev put her slightly smaller foot onto the impression. She slid her foot forward lining her toes up and pressed down slightly, squeezing a little water to the sides. Taking a deep breath, she stepped forward to the joggers next footprint and paused.

This small distraction from the terrible events that very well may ruin her life dreams, didn't last too long and reality began to creep back in. She could feel tears welling up in her eyes and quickly scanned the beach for passersby that might notice. Her foot pushed off the sand to reach the next footprint, when she felt a hard object protruding into the ball of her foot. Without much interest, she knelt down and dug her fingers into the sand to retrieve the offending article.

Pulling up a sort-of-round, flat rock, she brushed it off to see not a rock at all. A feeling shot through her entire body. No thinking, just an emerging sense of something. She wrapped her fingers around the object and walked down to the water. Bending down, she let a wave ripple over her hand knocking some of the sand from the object. It was a coin and she could make out some letters and images on its surface. It was not circular like the doubloon from Grandpa, but odd shaped, slightly out-of-round. As the caked sand fell away, she could see a cross on one side, some writing around the edges, and could make out an almost worn-away number, 1724. Flipping it over, a shield, the signature design of early Spanish coins, was clear to her with the number "8" beside it. Tossing it in the air, she laughed out loud, and knew right away; she held a silver Piece of Eight from 1724.

When the coin landed in her hand, she felt a jolt as her fingers closed around it. Then she heard a piercing rumble. Looking up, the receding light on the distant horizon became a viewing screen for visions that flashed in front of Bev's eyes. She saw eighty-pound silver bars skidding across wooden planks, boxes of coins spilling out and scattering, large troves of jewels strewn randomly in all directions. Screams and wailing filled her ears, that caused her knees to weaken, and she collapsed on the sand. Bev felt a blinding wind giving her the sensation of being pushed flat on the sand. Her hair seemed to comply and was flapping in these gusts of crushing winds.

After what seemed like forever, the coin dropped from her hand, as the noises diminished and the visions slowly faded away. Bev was horrified by the sounds ringing in her ears and the visions of a terrible event that could not possibly involve her. *What brought this on? Who was that jogger? Where did he come from? Was he real, or some sort of ghost? I don't believe in ghosts!* Her mind raced. *I've held many pieces of eight; none of them did this. Grandpa would have told me; Mom would have....* Bev stopped, stood up, and looked north onto a virtually abandoned beach, with only the pounding of the surf filling the airwaves. Then she looked south toward Miami. The jogger was gone.

She picked up the coin, and holding it between her thumb and forefinger, gently rubbed it to feel the contours stamped into the surface. *Who were those people? Why am I seeing them? This coin was made three hundred years ago...why...why.*

The sun had dropped behind the horizon, but there was still a touch of light that guided Bev back to the wooden gate. As she laid her hand on the latch, she felt the tension and even the urgency of life on Wall Street, Bitcoin, and all the rest start to melt away. Layers lifted from her mind. Those frightening visions on the beach came out of nowhere, but somehow cleared the way for a fresh look at...at everything.

She walked in the condo, tossed the coin on the table, poured a large glass of Sauvignon Blanc, and plopped down in a big chair. Her mind wondered to boundaries she'd been living with, limitations she grew up with, the people around her, and most of all the kind of person she wanted to be. She was feeling a new sense of openness, almost a new freedom encircling her.

Let's start cleaning this mess up tomorrow, she thought.

CHAPTER
EIGHT

Mathias put the land-line phone back in the cradle, sat back, and gave a sigh. Walter had agreed to meet him tomorrow at noon. An early morning departure would get him to the farm in Valdosta on time. He twirled the last swallow of Jack Daniels around in the glass, and finished it off.

Mathias arrived twenty minutes early, and parked on the side of the road before turning into the long driveway to the house with the map in the seat next to him. He was surprised that he felt somewhat lighthearted and thought, *Okay Walter and I will have a friendly, but pointed discussion, but we're going to get to the crux of the matter.*

When they sat down to talk, pleasantries lasted a few minutes, then Mathias said, "Walter, this map is a little stranger than I thought it would be. Are there things you aren't telling me about it?"

"Agreed. It's an interesting artifact. I wondered if you'd find it intriguing or just throw it in a corner and forget it," he said.

"It's more than interesting," Mathias said. "Are there things you should be telling me about it?"

Walter told him the origins of the coins and the ship wreck and then Mathias asked, "Go over the particulars of how you acquired the map again."

Walter sat back in his chair, "Tearing down that hotel addition was harder than we thought, and cost more than the developers were prepared for, but we got it done. One morning a demolition crew supervisor friend of mine, brought the map over to me," Walter explained, "Said a worker found it hidden in a wall in what used to be the manager's office. I think he was about to trash it, but had a second thought."

"Did he have any idea what it was?" Mathias asked.

"No idea. He looked at it enough to recognize some utility in it. That's why he brought it to me. In fact, he laughed as he handed it to me and said something like, *Here's your pot of gold.*"

"Any idea why he would say that?" Mathias asked.

"Actually, there was a rumor that during construction of the addition, they dug up an old pirate chest of Spanish gold and silver coins. The story went that the construction manager kept it and hid it somewhere with plans to later move out of the area so spending it wouldn't be conspicuous," Walter said.

"Just the map? No coins though?"

"All I saw was the map," Walter said.

The conversation trailed off as they sat down to lunch on the screen-porch.

Then Walter asked, "Are you making any use of the map?"

Mathias looked up. He thought about the right way to respond and how to pose the real question, and the real reason he was here.

"Did you get involved with the map, Walter?" he asked. "It has some strange qualities…I mean it's a weird thing, this map."

"Where has it taken you? Any caves?" Walter asked.

Mathias sat; his mind temporarily blank. Then he thought about a response, but no words passed through his lips. His mind raced. *Walter knew all along about the dangerous spell this map has on a person. He asked about the caves...he knows...knows more than he's saying. What else did he know and not tell me. Does he know the map changes? Did the map talk to him?*

Mathias seethed with a rage and anger welled up inside him. He felt like he wanted to tear Walter apart with his hands, piece-by-piece. It was not greed, or frustration, or any of those. It was pure rage! *Walter tricked him, putting this ticking time-bomb front and center into his life.* Walter didn't give him a choice; he rid himself of a virus, a sickness; and now it was he, Mathias, who carried the weight.

The silence lingered and Walter felt the tension build. He saw Mathias's complexion changeover to a red hue and his eyes start to bulge. He shifted in his chair, not knowing how to respond as a touch of fear crept onto the porch and settle in the space between them.

"This is cheating; no it's deceit!" Mathias's voice bellowed. "You knew the power of this map. The power on a man's mind, and you gave it to me anyway, with no warning, no civilized explanation. I can see it in your eyes; you want it back. I know you want it, but you're not getting it now. It's mine and I'm going to find it...the treasure, and it will be all mine, and I'll bask in the riches, and do whatever I want in this world, and you won't get a dime, or a piece of eight, or one of your precious doubloons." Mathias rose from his chair with a sharp push off, bringing him to his feet quickly.

Walter's hands bolted to the arms of the chair, and his feet steadied. He was ready to jump up in fighting position to meet Mathias. Walter was 79 years old and hadn't seen a fight materialize for many decades, but like riding a bike he hadn't forgotten the hard knocks of growing up in a tough neighborhood. He was half a foot taller than Mathias, grew up a country boy, and still did a lot of the work on his farm. His hands were big, and he still figured that one good punch to the head of a smaller man would get him out of most battles.

Walter's forearms tensed, but just before he rose, Mathias grabbed the map, turned and sprinted through the screen door toward his truck. Walter walked to the doorway as he watched the dust cloud follow Mathias's truck out to the county road... and gone.

CHAPTER
NINE

The next morning Bev stood and stared into an empty hallway as the elevator door opened into the building lobby. She stopped at the red oak coffee service table, lifted a paper cup and watched it fill with the black liquid. She brushed her way past the doorman and into the open-air parking lot, and with a click of the key-fob, opened the door and slid into the driver's side. She pulled out, turned right and was on her way to wherever this Palm Beach road wanted to take her. Heading north, she veered right, onto the coast road, with a view of the beachside mansions. Her eyes trained on the oversize homes, but she didn't see them, just like she missed seeing the seagulls, the tourists and everything else. The visions from the beach were back, snippets of screams, the roar of the wind, the feeling of massive chaos. She was driving to get away, to leave it behind, but instead the dark cloud of pandemonium was following her and invading her every thought.

Driving into Palm Beach town center, she stopped at a light, looked up and finally noticed where she was, what she was doing. She'd been there many times but still it caught her by surprise, as if she were seeing it for the first time in a new light.

How did these big buildings get into this small beach town? OMG. It's not right, she thought.

Emerging from the short tunnel into West Palm Beach, she meandered north, becoming aware that the darkness in her mind was beginning to fade. Then she haplessly pulled into a small parking lot next to her mother's favorite coffee shop. A petite girl equipped with a bouncy-blond ponytail, not much younger than Bev, placed a large cream-colored ceramic cup, as much a bowl as a cup, on the two-top table, brimming with a cafe latte.

By the time the latte was finished, and more than an hour had passed, Bev rose from the table. She walked up to the short-squatty Subaru wagon that her mother leaves parked at the condo. Reaching for the door handle, she touched it, then turned away and spontaneously started to stroll down the wide sidewalk of Cocoanut Row. She crossed Whitehall Way and could feel her body relax and feel some of the trauma of yesterday's walk on the beach melt away. Even the Bitcoin fiasco and the lost million dollars slipped from her thoughts...for now.

Then Bev stopped and felt something that drew her attention, something so subtle that she almost missed. It was a tingle in her bones, a flavor in the air, a low rumble that she couldn't quite recognize. In a shuffle-like, meandering stride, she took a step onto a wide entry walkway, and followed the brick promenade into the grounds of the Henry Flagler Museum.

She'd toured it before with her mom and dad and Branson years ago, but with little to no interest. *Who cared*, she thought then. *I guess Henry liked it...some columns and big rooms, and what about that staircase...okay when can we get out of here.* But Bev saw everything differently today...today, the beginning of the new, everything new.

She stood in the doorway, looked at the grand entrance, and

felt like she was walking into a fantasy, dreaming herself to be a grand-lady entering a grand ball with the richest, most important people in the world, a world where opulence has no bounds. She stroked one of the marble columns with her hand, while contemplating the details of the life-size statues populating the entrance. The dark cloud of this morning seemed to fade away and be replaced by the wonder of all possibilities.

She wandered the rooms and byways and let the museum headset explain the details, and history of this famous house. The tour ended at the gift shop. The crowd was thin this time in the morning, so she easily browsed the shelves.

Suddenly a door opened, a door that had been barely noticeable. A young man emerged and quietly passed by her. She stepped closer and saw a small latch handle tucked in flat against the door. Turning a complete circle to scope out the room, she saw nobody looking her way, and nothing keeping her hand from reaching for the latch. Slipping through the doorway, she found herself at the top of a narrow staircase. The light was minimal but adequate to show her the way down to the open hallway below.

BEV WALKED SLOWLY down the hall, cautious not to look out of place if she ran into someone. She stopped as she noticed a shadowy hallway on her left. Looking both ways, she made the turn and started off down the new direction. Just then, voices and a faint murmur of music seeped into the air around her. Suddenly the light brightened and banks of small offices appeared on both sides. One or two people looked up from their desk to scope out the stranger, but the vibe was casual and laidback.

She kept walking as the hall ended into a wide-open room that appeared to be made of poured concrete and painted a hospital-gray color. The temperature dropped a few degrees and the cooler air had a musty, kind of older smell. A table with four chairs, a small grouping of lounging chairs, and four or five folding ones leaning against the wall, occupied the room. She felt isolated standing there, but also had an uncanny feeling of security. Not security as in a sanctuary in this cold empty room, but more like a relief.

She sat down at the table, took a few deep breaths, and laid her head on her folded arms...another deep breath...and rest. A few minutes passed when she looked up with a start to see a short gentle-looking man in overalls with a gray mustache. He smiled and Bev tried to reciprocate that friendly look before blurting out a big, "hi."

Through his gentle-old-man smile, he said, "A young lady taking a rest. How nice to see."

"It's been a long day," she said.

"Well at least a long morning," he replied. "We just turned the corner into afternoon, Princess."

Bev looked him straight in the eyes and for a spit second felt like *that* little girl, that princess with the wispy fairy dress. A princess without a care in the world.

"Hi I'm Bev and I got a little lost down here. I hope it's okay," she said.

"Looks like everything is fine, Miss Bev," he replied. "What brings you down to our little, private dungeon?"

"I guess I'm the curious sort. You could say I took a wrong turn," Bev said. "What's your name?"

He broke out into a deep chuckle at the "wrong turn" comment, then recovered and said, "Clive Andrew Mullens, but everybody calls me Butch."

"Butch, is this room an older part of the building? It's

cooler; there's a different scent in the air, and it has a different vibe?" Bev asked.

"So you have a 'vibe' going Miss Bev?" Butch said. "Well you're right, it's a different part of the building, but it's actually newer. After Henry Flagler, the original owner of the house, fell down the front stairway and died, new owners built a ten-story hotel addition in back, toward the canal. Later, that addition was torn down, but this part of the basement stayed for storage of water and electric utilities."

"Butch, you sound like the official historian around here," Bev said.

"I'm the head of maintenance, but I've picked up a few tidbits along the way, Miss Bev," Butch said.

Bev felt a warm, confident feeling all over, but could feel a mild anxiety beginning to seep into the room.

"I'll bet there are a lot of stories from the old days that go with this building," Bev said. "Stories about intrigue with the people, and even romances. I'll guess these walls know it all. What's the best story these walls could tell?"

"There's a rumor that Flagler's niece was actually his daughter, he had out of wedlock, before he married her mother."

"Okay, that's a good one," Bev said.

"Everybody's gossiped about that one, but there's another one I like. People say there was a pirate treasure hidden in the walls of the addition, and when it was torn down, this box of gold and silver coins vanished, but a map was found leading to its hiding place," Butch said.

Anxiety flooded into the room and visions filled Bev's mind. It was the wild wind and screams again, but milder and distant this time. This time the visions were of bigger-than-life coins shining and glaring, dancing before her eyes, and she fell back into the chair. Butch saw her and thinking she might faint, grabbed her elbow, helping her sit.

"Are you all right, Bev," Butch whispered.

Bev didn't reply, but sat with her eyes wide open staring at the visions of the coins...the ghost of long-ago treasure. Butch handed her a bottle of water and pulled up a chair next to her.

The visions receded, and finally Bev could focus.

"I'm okay. Just a bit dizzy. Maybe I'm getting a virus or the pandemic is back," Bev said, as she tried to muster a reassuring giggle. "Is there more to that story?"

"I'm sure there is more, but I never paid much attention to it. There is an old guy named Walter, who was supervising the tear-down, and his name is always mentioned when people talk about that story," Butch said. "Walter Talon, that's it. I used to see him around, back-in-the-day, but that's all I know. Hear he retired and moved to a farm in Georgia."

Bev sat back in the chair and took a deep breath...and then another. The visions gently faded away, and she sat staring at the gray walls. Butch stood up and with slow, measured steps walked to the hallway and disappeared. Bev hardly paid attention to Butch or anything in the room, and was lost in wispy thoughts of confusion and trepidation.

After a while, Bev noticed that Butch was quietly sitting next to her.

"Oh hi. Sorry I'm a bit lost in thought," she said. "Is everything okay?"

"I hope so. How are you feeling?" he asked.

"I don't know what happened just then," she said.

Bev felt disoriented and confused with these random visions that plagued her. She beckoned her other persona, her Wall Street business personality, the one that was shiny and slick, to jump in and save face.

Then feeling back on track she said, "Anyway, that's a really fun story about the treasure buried here. Does anyone really believe it?"

"Show me the goods is my motto…believe it when I see it," he said.

Bev smiled and felt the urge to stand. When she did, Butch quietly stood next to her.

"Well for what it's worth, I found a phone number for Walter. I don't know if he's still upright, or living in Georgia, or what, but if you want to know more, you can call," Butch said.

Bev tried hard not to show her surprise, took the piece of paper, and slipped it into her back pocket.

CHAPTER
TEN

After making her way back to the condo, Bev sat down in the big chair on the deck overlooking the ocean. She dialed Walter's number expecting the ringing phone to jump to voicemail, when a voice crackled through her cell phone.

"Walter here. What can I do you for?"

Bev stammered a bit, being caught off guard. She looked out to the eastern horizon, over the Atlantic, as the filtered rays of the early afternoon sun warmed the south Florida coast.

"Mr. Talon, I'm Bev Dennison and I have an interest in the story of the treasure hidden in the walls of the Flagler Museum. I know it's most likely a rumor or even just a myth, but the story intrigues me and someone said you know the most about it," she said and took a deep breath after that mouthful. Without thinking, she used her mother's maiden name instead of her own last name, Dahl, for this introduction.

Walter let the fleeting thought of a problem go by, but did not speak immediately. A smile grew on his face and he knew that many people over the years had been fascinated with the story of this treasure. He didn't bother to think past that.

"Miss Dennison, everybody in Florida wants to find that pot and get rich quick," he said. "I appreciate the call, but you're going to have to find all that treasure on your own."

Bev stammered a bit and knew this call was about to end.

"Mr. Talon, was there a map that ever surfaced to this treasure? I know it wouldn't be anything important, but more of a curiosity or artifact." she said.

Walter did not answer. He pulled the iPhone away from his ear and looked at the screen as if to get perspective, or see who he was talking to, but really to let some space into the conversation.

He mustered a deep chuckle and said, "Like I said, getting rich quick is fascinating, and artifacts and maps and all of that is fun to think about. It's been nice talking to you."

Walter let his voice drop as he finished, signaling the conversation was nearing a close.

"Did this map ever change or show points on it that moved or transitioned?" she asked. "Mr. Talon, if the map did those things, I may have some information about it."

The low crackle of the phone line was the only sound between them, but the explosion in Walter's head was shattering. He pushed back in his chair and thought about what to say next, but no words would fit into the onslaught of emotion. Then a pang of fear bolted through him like a lightning bolt in a summer storm. *How would she know about the map, and who was she anyway?*

Then Bev broke the silence, "I could drive to Georgia and be there in the morning to have a casual discussion about this."

Still Walter sat there hardly moving a muscle.

"I'm in the Islands, Miss...Miss Dennison," he said.

"Oh, the Islands?" she quizzed.

"Virgin Gorda," he said.

"If you'll agree to see me for an hour, I'll be there tomorrow afternoon," she said.

Bev blurted it out as a last-ditch effort, but expected her proposal to be declined. Her mind flashed back to Christmas and the card from cousin Mathias. The map that lit up when she looked at it. *Okay after he hangs up, maybe I'll call my mother. Maybe I'll sit here next to the Atlantic Ocean and do nothing, or maybe...*

"Three o'clock tomorrow, Miss Dennison. I live at the top of the mountain overlooking North Sound on Virgin Gorda. Can you find it?" Walter said.

"Yes I can. Do you look down at the red roofs of Leverick Bay?" Bev asked.

"Yes that's it," he said.

"See you at three," she said and started to reach for the off button on her phone.

"One more thing, Miss Dennison." Did you know a treasure hunter named Richard Dennison," he said.

"Yes, he was my grandfather."

THE THREE-HOUR FLIGHT from Palm Beach airport landed at eleven-fifteen in the morning. Bev took the hand of the co-pilot as he offered to help her down the four short steps to the concrete tarmac at Beef Island airport on the east end of Tortola in the British Virgin Islands. There was one other passenger on the two-engine, eight-seat private jet. He darted ahead of Bev down the steps. Bev slung her overnight bag over her shoulder and walked into the terminal to the customs counter.

The five-minute walk to the pier at Trellis Bay was a familiar stroll for her as was the fiberglass cigar-boat with twin 300 horsepower outboard engines waiting at the pier. She looked out over the bay, past the naked masts bobbing on anchor in the breeze, and could see the small, round island of Marina Cay, and the petit, white sand beach where she and Branson played as kids. Grandma Jennifer had a house and sail boat there. Mom and dad would do the work of sailing the boat, but grandma was a better sailor, so she was in charge on the water. Sometime during her high school years, the family trips there trailed off, but Bev was so caught up with teenage stuff, she didn't really notice. Still she got a chill of nostalgia just getting a glimpse of the island.

On arrival at Leverick Bay, a stubby little dented-up gray Honda waited for her in the parking lot. She grabbed her favorite lobster sandwich at the walk-up counter in the small provisioning store, leaving her about an hour to make the trip to Walter's house.

WALTER SIPPED from his morning coffee cup and starred out over the bay. He had tossed and turned during a fitful night. Lying on his left side, he resolved that he would be guarded with Bev, *not say too much. What good would it do him? What good would it do her? This was a dead-end, a fool's dream...a fabulous folly.*

As he turned and rolled over to his right side, he was sure he wanted to tell her everything, completely unload this burden, be done with it once and for all, pass it to any fool who'll take it. *I thought I passed it to Mathias. Why is it coming back to me? Richard Dennison's granddaughter...does she know something I don't. I don't want all these riches,* he thought.

He woke up exhausted.

Seeing the beat-up little car bouncing down the long driveway, he checked the screen door next to the parking area at the front of the house. *Yep, it's open.* Then he walked back to the living room, sat and stared at the panoramic view over the bay a thousand feet below.

He answered the knock on the door by shouting, "Come on in."

After two hours talking to Walter, Bev pushed open the screen door and slid behind the wheel. She pointed the car down the curvy road to the small marina at Leverick Bay. She parked and ascended the stairs to the outdoor patio-seating overlooking the Bay, where she comprised a crowd of one. Sipping on a bottle of Carib beer, she sat quietly contemplating a story she had never expected.

Finally, she picked up her phone and clicked on "Mom" in the favorites. She had too much to tell her for one conversation, so the Bitcoin disaster would have to wait.

Alice answered and Bev started, "Hi Mom, I know I've been remiss in calling lately. It's just a lot is going on."

"Really. Good to hear your voice," Alice said following her normal strategy of being neutral to see what spills out on the other end.

"Mom, did you ever meet a man from Florida named Walter Talon?" Bev said.

"No, it doesn't ring a bell. Why?" Alice said.

"He knows who grandpa Richard was, along with everything about that treasure you and dad found on Marina Cay. He also knows cousin Mathias...says he entrusted him with a map. Mom, Mathias might be obsessed with that map. That one in his last Christmas card was strange," Bev said.

"Grandpa and his quirky clues got a reputation after we found the coins. As far as Mathias, well, I haven't really seen him in years. Is he getting along okay?" Alice said.

"Mom, remember at Christmas when I saw that map light up and some lines move?" Bev said.

"Not really dear. It was just the uneven light from the windows," Alice said.

Bev took a breath, not sure how to say this, "Mr. Talon came apart in front of me. First, he got red-faced and then pleaded with me to not involve him. He gave a map to Mathias that had led him in and out of caves, and now Mathias is overboard on this, and even threatened Mr. Talon," Bev said.

"That doesn't sound good. I'm sure it can't be that bad. I'll call Mathias and get a feel for the situation," Alice said. "Are you still in Palm Beach?"

Bev paused while her eyes darted around the restaurant/bar, then she looked out to the Virgin Island's most breathtaking bay, and with a guilty feeling said, "Yes."

CHAPTER
ELEVEN

The seatbelt sign lit up on the Southwest Air flight into Nashville, and the captain's voice came over the speakers, "Please take your seats and the attendants will be by to collect any remaining trash. We know you have choices when flying..." Bev looked out the window as the plane banked right to approach the airport. She could see the Cumberland River snake through its tree-lined path and wobble past Nissan Stadium and the skyline of Nashville. She wondered if there'd be time to visit the famed Country Music Hall of Fame, or the hundred-year-old Parthenon replica near the city center. If she had time, first on her list was a stroll down Broadway to experience the cowboy-boot-short-skirt-Bud Light culture that was iconic and famous in Nashville.

Rolling to the gate, Bev took her phone off airplane mode, and punched the "Mom" button.

"Are you sure it's okay for me to visit cousin Mathias?" Bev said when her mother answered.

"Look dear, it'll be just fine. I had a long chat with him, and he's excited to see someone from our family visit him. Besides I told him you are looking around for places to live if you leave New York," Alice said.

"Did you mention anything about the treasure map?" Bev replied.

"Not exactly. Mainly because I don't know much about it, really nothing about it. But I did say you were intrigued with his Christmas cards," Alice said.

"What did he say?"

A smile inched onto Alice's face and she was tickled that Bev was still showing this mysterious sense of intrigue that engulfed her as a young child. She had warned Mathias that Bev was a sweet child, but a bit whimsical.

"He said he's looking forward to meeting you," Alice said.

MATHIAS STOOD on the doorstep as Bev pulled into the driveway. With a noticeable pep-in-his-step, he walked to the driver's side and opened the car door for Bev.

"So glad to see you, Bev. I've heard so many good things about you and your Wall Street career," he said. "We're a little simpler down here, but we get by."

Bev had heard the humble-pie dialogue before, but the southern version was nicer, and she kind of liked it. Did it feel more inclusive or just warm and fussy? She didn't know.

"Honestly, I came here with my family for visits, but it was a long time ago and I was just a little kid. Mom always told Branson and me that if we get the chance visit the relatives in the South; you'll probably learn something. So here I am," Bev said.

On the drive out of Nashville and into the suburbs, Bev passed houses on the small road after leaving the four-lane, but the scenery progressively changed to fewer houses and more trees and fields. She stood in the driveway, turned a half-circle and looked around; *five or six acres*, she thought.

Mathias led the way onto the wide porch which was shaded from the noontime sun. Bev stood there for half a second to feel a cool breeze blowing through a porch designed to capture that breeze. They went into the house and settled into the large, high-ceiling, front sitting room. The furniture appeared antique and each piece was unique with rich, wood finishes and classic southern fabrics.

Mathias glanced at the center table to make sure the Christmas card was open and facing Bev, and in the far corner he peered at the real map rolled up and leaning against a chair just as he had placed it, in case he needed it for backup.

Bev's keen eye scanned the room and noticed the Christmas card, but made sure her gaze didn't linger there so as not to reveal her interest. Meeting strangers is always a positioning exercise even if it's family, but Bev was more comfortable with these social niceties after her brief tenure in New York and the necessity of interacting with colleagues and customers.

How is your mom? Is your dad getting along okay? Do you miss California? Is Branson settling in to California? Tell me all about Wall Street... all the usual small talk.

What a lovely house and setting. Have you lived here long? Are you retired now? Are things settling down after aunt Kathy's passing?

All the answers were as formulaic as the questions, as they worked through them. By then, Bev could feel a distant tension, though more of a rumble or a kind of buzz. It didn't feel like danger, but a newness...of possibilities...of opportunity...of expectation. She stopped for a split second to wonder what these feelings were all about, but as quickly let it go. *Is this what people called a "sixth sense,"* she thought.

Bev had questioned her mother about it a while back. Her mother stopped, became quiet and then said, that she understood, but to just call it intuition for now. Her mom looked out whimsically into the room and repeated, intuition for now, just intuition.

AS THEY SAT and ate the light lunch Mathias served, Bev noticed a ray of blue light peaking from under the Christmas card that was lying on the coffee table. She turned an eye in that direction and as casually as she could, looked to see if Mathias noticed the map lighting up. He didn't show any sign of it; his gaze was trained on her. He was keeping an eye out for any reaction Bev may have to the card and map it contained.

She gave no ground in this standoff, but decided now was the time to drill down to the crux of the matter.

"Mathias, I enjoyed looking over your Christmas card last year. Mom tells me you have a fascination with maps. How interesting," she said.

Mathias spoke quietly but Bev could feel his continuous razor-focus-stare at her.

"An old friend I met during my work career in Florida got me interested in maps and it's proven to be a fun hobby," he replied.

"Do you collect old maps and tie them into adventures from history?" she asked.

"Today most maps seem to be roadmaps, following the asphalt around. I know people buzz around, so today maps are very practical. My interest is off the beaten path. That's where the intrigue is," he said.

"Sounds like fun," Bev continued the social niceties,

bantering around and hopefully weaving into some crevice in the armor that would lead to the real questions.

Mathias leaned back into his chair and took a deep breath. Bev felt the ice breaking between them and was sure the story was about to unfold.

"I wasn't really looking for a hobby and didn't know anything about treasure or treasure maps. That friend from Florida was kind of a wise older man in the construction business, and through our casual friendship, he gave me a map that is maybe a hundred years old," he said. "I thought it was very nice of him and threw it in the back seat of my truck where it sat for weeks. One day I was digging around back there and came across the map. After dinner I unrolled it on the kitchen table and thought it looked interesting."

Bev was not seeing, in front of her, the frantic, out of control man that Walter Talon was describing in his living room on Virgin Gorda. This was a calm and gentle soul with an interesting story to tell. Bev sat back and began to let her guard down and felt comfortable in his presence.

"What was this older man's name?" Bev said, wanting to get clarity.

"He was kind of a guru of construction down around Palm Beach. His name is Walter Talon," he said.

Bev paused to think about this and then said, "So he's still alive?"

"Yes he is. Retired though."

"Well Mathias, what did you do with the map at that point?" Bev asked, satisfied with moving on to Mathias's story.

"I tried to get some context by looking for familiar places, or landmarks, really anything that would orient me. I finally recognized some caves in the area not too far from here. Let me show you what tipped me off," he said.

Mathias cleared the coffee table including the Christmas card, walked over to the corner and grabbed the map, itself, and rolled it out over the table. As he did, Bev saw prominent lines on the surface start to light up. The crisp edges of the lines began to sizzle and vibrate. Out of the corner of her eye she snuck a glimpse of Mathias to see if he noticed, but he showed no sign that anything was happening out of the ordinary.

Without meaning to, Bev brought the palms of her hands to her eyes and rubbed, slightly messaging each eye as if they needed a rest. Mathias stood and watched with a slight smile forming on his face. He was not looking at the map, rather he was focused on Bev and appeared to be reveling in her observations.

Finally she looked up after marginally recovering and said, "Interesting map. I can see why you got intrigued with it.

Mathias pointed to an illustration that vaguely looked like a simple line drawing of a cave and as he did, Bev could see slight crimson illumination on it which appeared to her to be alternating between pulsing and fading away.

"This bend in the river crossing this road, reminded me of the old Haynes Abbey Road, so I drove down there and asked around. One old guy knew of a cave entrance that he and his cronies played in as kids. I followed his directions with the map on the seat next to me."

He made a point of not saying anything about the map lighting up or changing. His goal was to let Bev see what she could see. If she were the one person who could lead to the treasure, he would give her space and follow. She could turn out to be his guide to the treasure...*his treasure.*

Bev's questions led to Mathias telling her more about finding the cave and even his exploration of it. He didn't tell her about the few silver pieces of eight and gold doubloons he found scattered around an empty hole in the dirt.

At around four in the afternoon, Bev got in her car, backed out of the driveway, and headed back to her hotel in Nashville. She carried with her a mental picture of the map, a new insight into her nice, generous cousin, and an invitation to see the cave tomorrow morning.

CHAPTER
TWELVE

Price Davis walked past the crowded bar on the second floor of Tootsie's Orchid Lounge, and stepped up on the stage. He ducked slightly to pull the guitar strap over his head, looked back at his bass, drum, and lead guitar band mates, then turned to face the revelers. The band stood frozen in the moment as Price sang solo, *Your cheating' heart will make you blue, you'll sob and sob for a love that's true.*

The crowd erupted because Price was giving them what they traveled all those miles to see, old-favorite country songs while patiently slugging down copious amounts of Bud Light. The set list had Johnny Cash, Kristofferson, Hank Snow, and Willie on it, but he opened with the king himself, Hank Williams.

Meanwhile Bev strolled from her hotel down Fifth Avenue in Nashville until she hit the strip on Broadway. She stood next to the Bridgestone Arena, and looked at the stream of bodies; more cowboy hats than she thought even existed, miniskirts and boots. It brought a smile to her California-face. She pointed her phone down the street toward the Cumberland River...click. Then across the street to Tootsies, Roberts Footwear...click,

click. Swish, they're on the way to mom. The sun was setting, but the light would linger for another half hour. She crossed Broadway and walked past the long line snaking onto the sidewalk to get into Tootsies. Her pace slowed but she kept strolling down to First Street and a view of the river...Buy One Get Two Pair Free. What would she do with three pair of cowboy boots? Click, off to mom. Oh what the heck, send it to Branson too.

She turned around at the Hard Rock Cafe and started back up the sidewalk. Across the street, Kid Rock's Big Ass Honky Tonk and Steak House. Click...swish...sent. *The Bud Light is the same in every bar. I wonder if Kid is hanging out with the guys over there? Yeah, right. I don't know about this scene, maybe the hotel bar and a nice glass of cold wine?*

She crossed Fourth Avenue heading back to the hotel, and veering into the street to get around the expected Tootsies line. But glancing over to see the doorman by himself, she noticed the line had dwindled. On impulse she darted over, presented her ID, and walked into the venerable bar.

Back in the day, the backdoor of Tootsie's opened to an alley and to the back stage door of the famed Grand Ole Opry House. It's just known as the Ryman Auditorium now because the Opry show moved to the suburbs. In the early days of radio, the show reached people for hundreds of miles to sell insurance products and everything else, featuring performers rotating on and off stage with short sets designed for the radio audience. In those days, the two tables in the back of Tootsies were a landing spot to wait while the broadcast weaved its way into the next set for Hank Williams, Uncle Dave Macon, Bill Monroe, Roy Acuff, Chet Atkins, Little Jimmy Dickens, and George Jones all crowding in at one time or the other. No Bud Light in those days, but Sterling Ale and PBR did the trick; stories told and songs written.

A tourist Mecca now, the visitors drain a few at the bar, and their ordinary little-town-workaday-life can seem to melt away. They can feel like they're on that stage, careening and blaring out those love-sick songs to ever adoring fans just like Hank did; at least till the next morning when their head is pounding and reality knocks at the door, some would say, just like Hank.

Bev slipped past the first bar through the narrow passage to the back bar. There are two stages on each floor, and the bar in the back was full, so she headed up the well-worn staircase. Peering over into the front room, she saw a few stray cowboy hats, but she felt no allure in that direction. Then she turned to see a crowd in back, and one empty seat at the bar.

Even Bev knew the sound of Hank Williams and she was sure a tall glass of something was in her immediate future. The band played softly so as not to drown out the words of the King as they floated across the room, *You'll pace and walk the whole night through, a heart that cheats will make you blue.*

Wow, she thought. *That guy delivers Hank lyrics better than Hank, himself.* And no hat. Brown hair falling over his ears, young face, bronze skin, probably older than he looks. She pictured Darien sitting next to her in this honky-tonk country music bar. No-way, no-how. Taking a deep breath, she settled onto the bar stool, all alone with a hundred other people.

Just the way people do, she found herself wondering what it'd be like dating that guy, the singer. A free-spirit, good looking, auto mechanic, or truck driver. A fling could work, it's a new life, what could it hurt, don't let mom know. She stopped and looked away and snickered, laughing at herself. *A couple of beers and you're a country cowgirl. Better get to the hotel while it's still early,* she thought. *You have a date with a limestone cave, a map, and cousin Mathias tomorrow.*

CHAPTER
THIRTEEN

Coffee and a small quiche were set on the front porch dining table. When Bev arrived at Mathias's house, cloth napkins, two forks, and hand-made porcelain plates were set out. Bev had wondered how Mathias was getting along after his wife died six years ago. The house had a "woman's touch" still, and by all accounts he was maintaining it. Two dogwood trees were in full bloom, one white near the house, and vibrant violet blooms on the other. The conversation was easy-going and light.

"Do you find the East a lot different from California?" he asked. "How is that fast pace New York City? And investment banking?"

"The east coast is different all right, but what I notice more than anything is the difference in people, especially here in the South," she said. "People seem to belong around here. You know what I mean? Belong to a place. At least in Silicon Valley there feels like an attitude of "take what you can get, while you can get it and leave the rest...or something like that. In New York there is a feeling of place, but it seems shallow."

"Interesting. I can tell you that it takes a while for new

people to settle down after they move here, but most do after a bit," he said. "And New York City for you?"

"Well Mathias, it's a bit of a story, but I'll just say that it's an exciting place that may not be the right fit for me."

"And what about all those people?" he asked.

"Yeah, way too many people in that small space."

The conversation meandered until Mathias reached for the map and rolled it out over the table. He secured the corners with salt and pepper shakers and water glasses. The minute he started unrolling it, Bev heard sounds. Not like on the beach when she stepped on that coin...more subtle...more like whispers punctuated with short beeps. She looked up at Mathias to see if he was hearing this, but he gave no sign of noticing anything. He was gazing down at the map, but his peripheral vision was trained on Bev.

He pointed to areas on the map as he told Bev about the caves.

"You probably have heard of the massive limestone cave system running through Tennessee," he said.

"Well, no Mathias, I never have. Tell me about it," Bev replied.

He gave her the five-minute primer on the longest cave system in the world running from southern Kentucky through Tennessee and into northern Alabama.

"The rainwater picks up carbon dioxide from the air which turns into a weak acid as it percolates through the soil. The acid slowly dissolves the limestone along the joints, fractures it, and over time, eats away the insides to form caves. The sandstone layer near the surface is not affected and a lot of times serves as a protective cap over the caves."

"How long does it take?" Bev asked.

"Maybe millions of years, but some are a hundred million or

more. So far they have mapped five hundred miles of caves in this system," he said.

Bev thought for a minute then looked down at the map, "Are they all connected?"

"Connections are being discovered as they explore more, so there are many connections that haven't been found out yet," he said.

Bev looked at the map again and could see a small area on the right side subtly move and slightly adjust its end point. Again she glanced at Mathias for a reaction, but saw none.

He pointed again to a spot on the map just below the changing section Bev witnessed, and began telling her about the cave that he'd been focusing on. She watched and listened as he unfolded the story. He explained how he'd found deep unexplored caverns near this very spot. Bev began to get an unsettled feeling, but couldn't tell where it was coming from. Looking at the map for clues, she saw none...no movement in the lines...nothing lighting up...just an uneasiness. Maybe this story wasn't all together true. She wondered if her cousin was embellishing or even fabricating some of his story. The uneasiness was oozing up from somewhere.

After breakfast Bev and Mathias climbed into his truck and started the trip to his secret cave entrance.

TX 1080 HD

SNW STUDIO

CNVFF

FILM SERIES

BEv

CHAPTER
FOURTEEN

That evening back in her hotel room in downtown Nashville, Bev kicked her shoes off. Some of the cave mud she tried to knock off earlier was still clinging to her running shoes. The thought of putting them in the bathroom to limit spreading the gray, damp mud occurred to her, but she blew it off as she punched a button on her cell phone and sat back in the chair.

"Hi Bev," her mother saw caller ID pop up.

"Wow Mom. I just had a tour of cousin Mathias's private limestone cave, and got an intro into his treasure hunt," Bev said.

Alice relaxed and took a deep breath...a treasure hunt. She flashed back to the feeling of the phrenetic time when she and Andrew pursued Grandpa Richard's treasure hunt in the islands. The worn-out cliche rumbled through her mind, *the best of times, the worst of times;* feeling the exhilaration of the hunt, the thrill of victory and the pain at the end. All their lives were turned upside down.

She pulled her focus back to her daughter, trying to remain neutral and said, "So Mathias is a treasure hunter now?"

"I can feel an obsession, but he is low-keying it. I'm not sure where he stands on this thing, or why he's telling me about it," Bev said. "Mom, remember when I asked you about the Christmas card map and some lights flashing on it?"

Alice said nothing.

Bev continued, "Mathias has a big map that he used to make the card we got. Mom, not only are some light flashes happening, but the lines of the map are moving a bit," Bev said.

Alice knew she was in delicate territory here. She sat still and said, "The lines are moving?"

"Yes, but what's throwing me off is that I'm getting feelings that seem to be dropping in on me, kind of like they belong to someone else. It's some pushing, some anxiety, it's unsettling," Bev said.

"And what are you doing about these feelings? I mean do you feel like this is compelling you to act or to react to them?" Alice said.

"A little bit, but mostly I feel flooded with information," Bev said.

Alice jumped in immediately, "You're doing the right thing. Watch and listen. Resist reacting."

"What is going on?" Bev asked.

"It's called clairvoyance, and it's perceiving information in other ways than our normal five senses; seeing, hearing, touching, smelling, taste," Alice said.

"Extrasensory?" Bev queried.

"It's sometimes called that, but the reality is it's perfectly normal. It's just not conventional, understood, or accepted by average people," Alice said. "If you're seeing a map move, you may be exceptionally gifted in clairvoyance or even psychokinesis."

"I didn't ask for this, Mom," Bev said.

"You don't ask for things like this, but you do have to learn to manage them. This can be very enlightening, but can be very dangerous," Alice said.

"Okay, okay, I'll be careful." Bev resisted the "be careful comments" because she thought her mother was shielding her, protecting her. She didn't need protecting. At twenty-three, she was a fully grown adult and this was just a fluky thing that she could handle.

Bev continued, "Funny thing, we had to squeeze through these really narrow rocks to get to his large cavern where there was an empty hole in the dirt, and where he found some coins... silver pieces of eight."

"He had actual coins in his hand?" Alice asked.

"Yes, and then he talked about the narrow entrance and how nothing much would fit through it...especially anything that would go into that empty hole in the ground," Bev paused enough for Alice to start to interject, but Bev cut her off.

"Mom, get this, I had a distinct awareness that the former contents laying in the dirt came from an entirely difference direction. Taking the flashlight, I looked for a passageway. I followed my instinct to the opposite wall and literally felt the opening, but Mathias shouted that it led nowhere, only a short offshoot."

Alice didn't try to say anything. She sat in her kitchen with the phone to her ear and waited for her daughter to exhaust her train of thought.

"Mom, I want to believe Mathias, but I know he's wrong," Bev took a breath. "Now I'll tell you this, but no comments, please. In my mind's eye, I could see shadowy figures moving through that part of the cave. I looked over at Mathias and got the feeling that he was not so much lying, but he simply did not understand what was going on. I wonder if that's why he's bringing me in on all this," Bev paused, "We're going back in that cave tomorrow, I'll let you know.

When the conversation ran out of steam and Bev said goodbye, Alice looked at her phone and punched a speed-dial button.

"CPRI, Jeanine speaking," the voice said.

"Hi Jeanine. You're just the person I want to talk to. This is Alice."

"Yes, Alice. I see a bit of anxiety in your space right now. It's kind of a cold muggy energy. Interesting," Jeanine said.

Alice took about five minutes to summarize Bev's situation to Jeanine at the California Paranormal Research Institute in Palo Alto.

"There's adventure in this for your daughter, and intrigue I'll add, but risk too. She'll need to sharpen up her game to get through this. Looks like Bev dreamed up this adventure for herself, or as we say she "mocked it up'," Jeanine chuckled as she delivered her reading of the situation. "Monotony collapses time; novelty unfolds it. She's young and feels in control."

"Any suggestions?" Alice asked.

"Does Bev have any training yet?" Jeanine asked.

Alice simply answered, "No."

"I'm seeing that she can move objects, Psychokinesis. It's fairly rare to see that. I'll go into trance and communicate with her on the Astral Plane...give her some information about her abilities. I feel like she's going to need it," Jeanine said with a final giggle.

AFTER SHE GOT BACK to her hotel, Bev walked down the south side of Broadway toward the river. At First Street, she hopped up the steps to the Hard Rock Cafe to get a table. Waiting to be seated, she saw mostly an empty room, so she turned went through the front door and scurried down the steps, heading back up

Broadway looking for a little more vibrancy. *Not Tootsies' again*, she thought. After ducking her head in Blake Shelton's Ole Red Bar, she resumed a steady stroll up the crowded street. A weak smell of stale beer permeated the atmosphere, but seemed kind of mild especially when matched against the often garbage aroma of her recent home, and the New York City streets.

Margaritaville had a solo singer in the window banging out some country cover songs. She stopped for a minute and watched him lay his heart out in front a single mic to a handful of strangers. A smile came to her face and she thought, *I love Nashville*.

And then there was Tootsie's. Right in front of her. She stopped, hesitated, then entered nonchalantly, jumping on a stool at the first bar. She ordered a Gerst Ale and watched the lead guitar riff on a solo for a few minutes. Then picking up the half-empty beer, she meandered to the back, up the stairs, kind of like she wasn't looking for someone. On the second floor, she turned left and gazed toward the front stage, then to the back stage. Taking a deep breath, and a swig of beer, she headed that direction. The bar stools were about half occupied and she was able to snag one near the stage.

"Let me know when you're ready," the bar tender said. "You know, for another beer."

"Yeah sure. I will," Bev replied. "Hey what's the singer's name?"

He peered up to the stage, "Price. I think it's Price."

"Just Price?" Bev queried.

"Nobody uses last names around here. Just Price," he said. "I'm Thornton...but everybody calls me Tommy. Where you from?"

Bev mumbled, *California* then turned to watch the band kick up "Get Rhythm" vintage Johnny Cash from the 1950's. She'd never heard it and was delighted to notice both her feet dangling from the stool, bopping up and down with the fast beat. She smiled and thought again, *I love Nashville.*

This strip of Broadway was the number one destination for bachelorette parties in the country, so Price Davis saw more than his share of girls from the stage. Still when he looked at Bev, there was something about this dark complected, stunningly pretty admirer with her eyes trained on him. Jet-black cropped hair, high cheek bones, perched on a stool with her back straight as an arrow. A far cry from the bleach-blond-cowgirl bachelorettes sending up drinks to the stage. He nodded to her and it seemed she acknowledged. On the next song, he jumped off stage for a couple of minutes during a guitar solo, but when he returned, her stool was empty. He scanned the room. Gone.

CHAPTER
FIFTEEN

The morning sun was beginning to break over the eastern hills as Mathias filled a coffee mug. He added skim milk and a sprinkle of cinnamon for flavor. He sat in the kitchen looking out over the back two wooded acres that shielded him from his neighbors. Taking a long first sip, a single, fledgling thought of the map and the treasure snuck into his mind. He tossed it aside and looked at the low light of morning, break through the trees, knowing he did not want to start the daily obsession that robbed him of all other thoughts.

That afternoon after he and Bev were set to return from their cave excursion, Mathias's stepson was going to stop by with some papers to sign. He *was trying to think of anything but the map,* but then without warning, he recalled himself raising his voice at Bev yesterday, about that tunnel in the cave being a dead-end...trying to control all things about the map, and his treasure. *No loose ends.* Then he thought, *this whole stupid treasure hunt is unraveling and the ends are frayed like an old rope.* He knew at his core, it was out of his control. His distant cousin, Bev, was in the cat-bird seat. She had the visions; she would find his treasure, and he'd be ready to take it. He knew all this, but she didn't...yet! At that particular moment, on his first cup of coffee, he knew that for now he had lost and the map was still in control...again! For now.

He too had been intrigued by the tunnel Bev favored, but had convinced himself that it led to nothing. He'd never seen or felt darkness like in that tunnel. The complete absence of light was profoundly terrifying. The cave was endless and the darkness too claustrophobic for anyone, he concluded. So he told Bev it went nowhere.

Now he sat, consumed, but had to admit to himself that Bev has a sensitivity beyond his, beyond normal people. He thought about the voice, *she will find the treasure or you will die trying.* Without thinking, he rolled out the map on the kitchen table, put an index finger on a line leading from the cave entrance and traced it pressing down like he was trying to squeeze answers from the paper. He glanced up for half a moment to the woods outside, noticed a slight breeze rumbling through the trees, and sighed, knowing he was getting nowhere on his own.

MATHIAS AND BEV bounced along in the truck, both feeling worn out and chilled after a long day. He had taken her to a hidden entrance to the cave network that looked more like a sink hole than a doorway. Four large, stacked limestone slabs laid horizontally and wedged into the turf. They were flanked by two diagonally strewn slabs on each side that guarded a small pit. The blackish-gray surfaces were partially covered in green lichens, not unusual to a passerby and not extraordinary by any means. Mathias found it by mistake when his old dog, Buster, was sniffing around, and wouldn't leave. At the time, Mathias doubled back to grab Buster and put him on a leash, but Buster disappeared into the darkness. Something was pulling him down the dark passage. *Must be a possum or woodchuck*, Mathias thought.

He fired up his light, crawled past the first rock and to his surprise entered a sizable cavern about ten feet from the entrance. He looked down at the lumpy footing to discover small mounds that he since surmised to be lime deposits that dripped from the ceiling. As he walked, the lumps grew bigger until he was walking around some that were two and three feet high. The tunnel took him deeper with each step and the lumps became stalagmites rising to the level of his shoulders. The dripping lime deposits began to cover some of the walls. He laid his hand on one, careful to inspect this jagged looking surface, but found it smooth to the touch like polished marble.

At one point, the air became still and clammy which gave him the willies. When the path looked like it would end, he shimmied up the side of a boulder and holding the light in one hand, inched down the other side. As he touched the ground, he felt a cool breeze giving him goose bumps...and then he looked straight ahead into the continued abyss and endless darkness.

Each time he would find a new tunnel, he consulted the map, drew it on a plexiglass overlay with colored markers, and watched for a sign from the map. On rare occasions the map showed some small signal that served to suck him into its reach a little bit further. At one point, he followed a new tunnel all morning by walking, crawling, and squeezing but couldn't find the end. He pulled out the map and with a light chalk pencil extended the path of the tunnel due north. No sooner than he got it on the paper, the line abruptly shifted a half inch to the east. Mathias blinked, shook the light and looked again. Yes, there it was laying still, heading northeast. He was in a frenzy for weeks and ordered every topographical and aerial map as well as researched every reference going back to ancient times. After all that, the only thing he could derive from that quirky move on the map was...nothing...nothing...nothing!

Yesterday was a warm-up, but he felt the clues in this cave were more promising. Now that Bev was here, his general plan was to shotgun the information to her and watch to see if any insights emerged. So he took her to the hidden entrance and walked her back into the dark tunnel. The lantern shined a glow on Bev sporadically, but in general there was not much watching when they got into the darkness, so he was satisfied with taking her there to see what happened next.

What no one could see deep in that cavern was the feeling that Bev had. When they stopped to rest before turning back, she looked into the darkness ahead and felt a quiet understanding, that morphed into thoughts of satisfaction, before growing into a mild feeling of elation. The goose bumps on her arms from the cool breeze disappeared like she had just slipped a fleece jacket around her body. There was a warmth, a knowing... a validating.

Her first fleeting thought was to scream to the world...*I've got it...I've got this sucker figured out.* Instead she stood there, took a contemplative swallow and said nothing. She was learning and becoming more aware of her abilities and how to manage them. The trip back was quiet and as Mathias drove, she starred out into the rolling Tennessee hills watching the sun sink into the western skies.

BEV SAT on the front porch swing nursing a glass of white wine after a long and muddy day. The sun was setting and light filtered through the large maple tree in the front yard. She saw a light blue Prius turn off the road into the driveway, and then looked up at Mathias.

"That's my stepson. He's my lawyer and he's got a few bank papers for me to sign. It won't take long; he's a nice guy," he said.

"Okay, while you're doing that, I think I'll go have another look at the map," Bev said.

Mathias stopped abruptly and felt his head freeze in place for a split second and then thought, *it's okay, I don't have to watch her every second.*

She unrolled the map on the kitchen table as her eyes inspected the outside edges for no good reason other than to get context, and take in the big picture before landing on any details. Everything looked good. She moved her focus to the cave entrance he first showed her. The lines of the map ended there at the entrance. She reached down and touched that ending point and as she did, a faint illumination became visible as the line extended itself deeper into the cave. The dark tunnel that Mathias claimed went nowhere, was the precise direction of the growing line.

She looked to the side and made a guess to where today's cave entrance may be located, and put her finger down on that spot. When she did the growing line drew still and ceased its advance. Bev drew herself inward, took a deep breath and stepped over to the back window. The violet blossoms of a lone dogwood tree danced in a light breeze just outside the window.

Back at the map, she glanced down and felt a bit of humor in the air. She chuckled under her breath and got a feeling she recognized as playful, like when she was a little girl down at the creek carelessly tossing rocks into the stream, with no care in the world. A smile grew on her face as she looked back down to see the line lighting up and moving in uneven concentric circles until it stopped a few inches from its starting point.

Bev reached no conclusion from this move; she didn't need to conclude anything, no thinking was necessary. She stood up straight, with a knowingness...a far superior understanding than a mere cognitive solution. She rolled the map back up with the unequivocal understanding that the tunnel moved vertically up, for how far she didn't know. What was the map hiding...she didn't know. But she did know where it went, and she did know where it started and that it was a loop ending at the hidden cave entrance they explored today.

Mathias's feverish study of the map over the past weeks had not yielded this information, so she knew that he was not aware of this loop or how close he was to the hiding place he lusted for. Could it be a trove of silver pieces of eight partnered with the shiny gold doubloons all waiting and shivering in that cold, damp cave? The map had revealed none of those answers to Bev. She composed herself and walked toward the front porch to rejoin her cousin.

BEV HEARD the men's voices, cleared her throat and opened the screen door.

Mathias said, "Oh hi Bev. This is my stepson, Price."

Price turned around to face Bev. The standard greeting on his face instantly faded and a look of bewilderment replaced it. Bev stopped and took a half-step back. Mathias squinted and started to say something, but only a stuttering sound passed his lips.

Finally, Bev broke the stalemate, "We've met, well not actually met. I've seen you, I mean him, on the strip. I mean at Tootsie's."

"We've run into each other, I think, not really met before," Price tried to recover the moment as gracefully as he could. "Pleased to meet you. I'm Price Davis, attorney at law, at your service.

Bev salvaged her composure, extended her hand and said, "I'm Bev Dahl."

"Nice to meet your cousin, eh Price?" Mathias poked.

"Why, yes it is," replied Price.

Mathias turned toward the screen door and said, "Everybody sit down. This calls for a little good cheer. I'll be right back."

Mathias disappeared into the house, then Price looked at Bev, "I noticed you at the bar in Tootsie's last night."

"Well actually I was there the last two nights," Bev said. "I guess lawyers front bands in honky-tonks in Nashville?" she said.

"Lawyers do a lot worse things in Nashville," Price quipped.

"A lot worse things in fifty states and all the territories," Bev joked.

They both enjoyed the light moment and laughed.

"I guess we're not technically cousins. Mathias married my mom and helped raise me after my dad died in a car wreck," Price said.

"Yeah, people like to call it family anyway. That'll be okay," Bev replied.

Mathias heard them talking and slowed up in the kitchen to give them some time to get acquainted.

"What brings you to Nashville?" Price asked.

"I'm taking a break to look around. I'm not making this too public, but I just quit my job in New York in investment banking. I've got four months left on my apartment lease and looking for a place to land," she said.

"You're from California, right?" he asked.

"I guess it'd be normal to float back west and pick up my life there, but I want to give things some time to incubate," she said. "The truth is, I've got some interest in this treasure map Mathias has."

"You mean the map that has consumed my stepdad and changed him from a normal guy into a crazed maniac?" Price paused. "Maybe it's not that bad, but he's talked himself into thinking he'll get rich if he finds what that crazy map leads to. He's thinking mega-rich, islands, yachts, you know, all that stuff."

"What makes you think there isn't a treasure there?" Bev asked.

Price leaned back in his chair and laughed out loud. "What makes you think there 'is' a treasure there. Or anything there? And, where is 'there,' anyway?"

His unpretentious, southern style was infectious and Bev found herself laughing along with this southern cousin of hers. She felt that happy-go-lucky-little-girl feeling again, and embraced the moment. She liked this porch. She liked this warm breeze. She liked this cousin. She forgot about the map.

CHAPTER
SIXTEEN

Bev set the eyeliner brush on the bathroom counter and turned her face left, then right for the mirror to see. *Looks good*, she thought. But then she stepped back and her arms dropped to her sides. *Here it comes*, she thought. The success she'd enjoyed all day of banishing every thought of investment banking, Darien, and the whole New York world, was breaking down. Her mind raced. *Was it really only a few short weeks ago that the walls caved in around her? Was it a knee-jerk decision to bolt from it all...was everything she worked for left dangling...swinging aimlessly from a light pole at the corner of Wall Street and Main Street?*

Minutes later she recovered from this mental onslaught, finished her makeup, and sat down next to the glass door to brush her short black hair. She looked out toward Broadway, in the direction of the two-story buildings on the strip of honky-tonks, but the view was blocked by a phalanx of new towering hotels. She took a deep breath and broke out crying, first a whimper and then a full-blown flood of tears...for her, for Darien, for Mom, Branson, and Dad...or for nobody and no reason. She just cried.

An hour later, Bev bounded down the stairs of her hotel, into the lobby and through the revolving doors. She opened the car door and jumped into the light blue Prius.

"Hey you look great," Price delivered the standard line that always is expected. And always timely.

"Thanks Price. I'm excited to be going out on the town in my new favorite city. What's on the docket for tonight?" Bev's delivery was light-hearted and almost giddy.

"There's a little outdoor restaurant in a small marina on the Cumberland River. It's easy going and a cool hang," he said.

"I'm up for that. What's it called?" she said.

"It's called the Holy Mackerel," he said.

Really, that sounds like some New Yorker named it... a little too poignant and a bit too cool, Bev started to say, but bit her lip and let that thought float into the smartass-graveyard.

Price greeted most of the staff with smiles and backslaps. Then they were seated at a table on the deck looking out onto the mighty Cumberland River.

Bev expected blue jeans and boots for this country music singer, but instead got a white polo shirt atop khaki slacks and leather slip-ons. She was watching him during his jolly greetings of the staff, trying to figure this guy out. The New York guys were always Wall Street, even on the weekends. Price Davis was a different breed.

"Tell me about New York and life in *the* city. I'm sure it's a long story," he said.

"Well, it's a little hard to say right now, but it was mostly a short story," she squirmed in her chair and ran her fingers through her hair. "I went to Stanford and always liked economics. Everybody there wanted to be an investment banker, so I landed on Wall Street," she paused. "But..."

Price broke in, "My Dad took me to New York a few times.

We visited his school, Columbia, and also NYU, but I was too young to take it all in."

"So what happened?" she asked.

"My best friend decided on a little Episcopal school up on a mountain a couple hours from here. The architecture is orchard stone with a gothic design flavor. Really cool looking. The Sewanee Mining Company gave them ten thousand acres on top of those hills a couple hundred years ago," Price paused and looked out over the water and around the marina. "Great hiking, but beer is the most popular pastime. I did pre-law but it was good to get back to Nashville after four years," he said.

"Some cozy sweetheart waiting?" She asked.

"Didn't happen like that. I came back and jumped into songwriting down on Music Row."

"A Nashville Cat?" she said.

"I had a tune go to twenty on the streaming charts. Dirks Bentley. Then Mom gave me a good talking to."

"And?" she asked.

"Vanderbilt Law School," he said. "I got hired by a small firm. My mentor there retired and I took over his practice. Pretty laidback. I keep my own hours."

Bev sat silently and let it all sink in. Then said, "Wall Street owns all your hours in a day...you get none."

"Really?" he said.

"Well it feels like it, anyway," she said.

They both chuckled as the second round of drinks arrived. After baskets of fried stuff and more beer, Price and Bev walked up the narrow metal stairs ascending to the parking lot. Weaving their way around the bending walkway, their shoulders brushed causing Bev to glance over at him. Price seemed unaware of this pivotal event in their budding relationship. Bev looked down and watched her feet lift onto each step, and thought, *okay...does he even care...I mean a touch like that is impor-*

tant...it happened spontaneously because we're here together... together is something...after all, we could be walking around alone... or with somebody else...I don't think he cares.

Price walked to the passenger door of the Prius, pulled it open and stood like the footman of a carriage in a fairytale dream. Bev embraced the moment sensing the chivalry of the South unfolding, that was nowhere present in the homogenous melting pot of Silicon Valley. *Maybe he does care,* she thought.

"Want to go on a short tour?" he asked.

"I'm your prisoner. Drive on," she replied.

The Prius pointed west and eventually worked its way over to the Natchez Trace Highway. They punched through the darkness for a while before Price began the audio portion of the tour.

"This was a trail pieced together from short routes, forged by migration of animal herds and Indian tribes. It's pretty much accepted that if someone knew how to follow it, it would take them from Mississippi to Canada," he said, letting his words float in the dark, cool air, while Bev mildly acknowledged.

"When this was all part of the North Carolina territory, people put a bridge over this part of the Harpeth River for a shortcut. It's not in use anymore, but you can still see it," he said.

He pulled over onto a wide shoulder in the road, stopped the car, and reached over Bev to point out the bridge. His arm leaned over and he ducked his head slightly to look out Bev's window as he pointed.

"Can you see it?" he asked.

His face was only inches from hers and though it was expected she'd look out the window, all she could think about was laying a face-plant on him. *Okay this is contrived...parking here in the dark...or maybe he doesn't care and he just likes that stupid bridge...what if he has a girlfriend...this is the south, don't be aggressive...be a Southern lady...Christ, what's a southern lady, anyway...does he even like me,* Bev thought.

She didn't turn her head toward the window and the bridge, and when he looked up to gage her silence, he saw her bronze cheeks reflecting a glow from the low light. He pulled back slightly, stopped, and then looked into her dark blue eyes. In the silence of the night, his lips found hers, lightly brushing against them, then lifted his head slightly. When their lips met again, she pushed into his kiss and simultaneously felt a strength and resolve race through her body. She repositioned her arm, careful not to initiate an embrace. *I'm a southern girl*, she thought, but it made no difference as his hand squeezed around her back, waist high, pulling her closer.

Price pulled away, "Well, how do you like this tour so far?" he said with a barely discernible smirk.

"I really like the history of this place, and this bridge is awesome," she replied, as he joined her in a robust laugh.

"You can park over there next to the curb and it'll be okay while you walk me up to the room," Bev said as they pulled up to the lobby entrance of the hotel.

Price complied without acknowledgment. They walked through the revolving door and his hand went instinctively to the small of her back with a light touch. At her floor, the elevator door opened, and they stepped into the hallway while she dug out her card key and found the slot on the door. She tossed her purse on the queen bed, kicked off her shoes and meandered over to the curtain to pull it across the glass door.

"Big day. I'm going to get moving; I'll call you," Price quietly whispered.

Bev stepped over to Price and said, "You can't get out of here that easy, Mr. Southern Gentleman."

He put his hand behind her neck, gently messaging the skin above her shoulders, but didn't pull her forward. She leaned in and brushed her lips on his with a casual swipe. He smiled, turned toward the door, then looked over his shoulder and said, "Call you tomorrow."

Bev slumped into a chair and looked at the bedside clock. A few minutes past eleven...nine o'clock in California. She reached for her phone pulled up the favorites list and punched "Mom."

Alice answered and said, "Hi dear, how is the Tennessee adventure going?"

Bev fixed her stare on the curtains but caught herself focused on her mother's thought pictures instead. She could see the questions that hung in the air like dust in a breeze, unspoken, but lingering. She wanted to tell her mom about the caves, the honky-tonks, and yes Price Davis, her almost cousin, but she needed to clear the air about New York.

"So first of all, I quit the investment bank, only a few months left on the lease, and Darien isn't my type after all, Mom. I mean he was my type in New York, but honestly outside of that bubble...well, it doesn't work."

Okay, Bev thought, *that's a mind dump in CliffsNotes style,* so she prepared to unwrap that summary package layer by layer for her mother. But to her surprise and relief, Alice absorbed it all in stride.

"Mom, Darien and all those bankers lived life like somebody was chasing them, just frantic all the time," Bev announced.

Alice flashed back to Grandpa's treasure hunt and how her nice husband morphed from a quiet, content poet into a frantic-somebody-chasing-me, gold digger.

After a pause she said, "Finding your place at the table in

life is the challenge, Bev, and finding the people that are right is the biggest obstacle."

Bev muttered a few syllables while she recovered her thoughts. But the myriad of questions for her mom, that pressed on her like a lead-weight when she called, were fading away, and she could feel a calmness ambling into her mind, to take their place.

Bev launched in, "Mom, my intuition is picking up on this treasure map and I'm getting clear pictures of what the map is pointing to. I don't think Mathias has the same abilities, while at the same time he is getting buzzed and more electric. But Mom, this electric thing isn't in a good way. It feels scary, and I don't know whether to be afraid or just let it go."

CHAPTER
SEVENTEEN

Bev woke up around six, but laid in bed trying to slow her mind and settle back into sleep with marginal success. She opened one eye and looked at the clock...almost seven. She forced her left leg from under the covers and onto the floor, with a sigh of relief and a grand feeling of accomplishment, relaxed and laid there in silence. Finally, both feet hit the ground and dragged her over to the Keurig coffee maker. With a hot cup in her hand, she opened the curtains and looked out over the Nashville cityscape.

Then she reached for her phone and searched for "Walter." Virgin Gorda was two hours ahead so, *give Walter Talon a call*, she thought.

Walter's answering machine rattled out the same old message, so she simply left her name, laid the phone on the bedstand and headed over for a coffee refresh. Car horns were not honking that time of the morning, but the trucks were rolling through the streets, downshifting, brakes squeaking, sliding doors slamming. Bev tuned it all off and just let her mind wander through the last few days...the last few weeks...the last few years.

Am I mellow because I met a really nice guy, or am I tense because I have a cousin that is drawing me into a wild adventure? Do I need a treasure hunt? Do I want to read a map that changes right before my eyes? Do I want to navigate a virtual flood of thoughts cascading all over me? What's it called, clairvoyance? She stood and walked to the dresser and then back to the glass door.

Finding my place at the table... do I have a place at the table in California...back home? I guess I like country music...is this country singer-lawyer really that mellow...is he after treasure too...Nah...no way...it is treasure, though...everybody likes to be rich...who do I trust...I think I miss home.

The ring of her cell phone pierced the loose veil of Bev's musings.

"This is Bev," she subconsciously reverted to her Wall Street voice.

"Bev Dahl the country music star, in Nashville?" the voice replied.

A smile eked onto her face as she recognized her brother's voice, "Branson, I'm glad you called. I could use a little touch from home base right now."

"I got that feeling and after I talked with Mom last night I woke up early thinking about you," he said.

"Then you know about New York? Darien? Investment banking?" she asked.

"Yeah, Mom spilled the beans on it all. She was a little vague on the bitcoin thing," he said.

"Okay." Letting that part sit for now. "All I can say is, ugly," She replied.

Bev filled him in by repeating most of the story she told their mom. He dutifully listened.

"So tell me about this cowboy you met," Branson said.

"Yeah, he's wearing boots, but there's no cowboy there. He's a good songwriter, but never had a breakthrough. It turns out that writing songs on Music Row is the easy part, but getting them on the radio is a bear," she said.

"Man, you sound like you're drinking the Kool-Aid down there," he said.

"Price says everybody wants to write songs here, and they arrive every day from some little town with stars in their eyes. He likes to say that you can't swing a dead-cat on Broadway without hitting a songwriter," she said.

"That phrase wouldn't make it past the PC police here in the Golden State. Maybe 'yawl' or 'awe shucks,' but not the dead-cat thing," he joked and joined Bev in a chuckle.

Then he said, "Slide into those new boots and shimmy on back to California. There's a big gala at the Fairmont Hotel in San Fran this Saturday, and as usual I don't have a date. We'll have a ball. Come on, say yes."

The conversation between brother and sister spread out wider and included Dad, Branson's long visits to Los Angeles, found treasure and more. Then Bev's phone pinged. She pulled it away from her ear and saw the new email notice; a ticket to San Jose tomorrow.

"Did you just buy me a plane ticket? She asked.

"Yep. I'll be seeing you and those new boots tomorrow," he said.

BEV HUNG up the call and looked in the closet. Nope, these aren't the right cloths for this jaunt to California. She would have to mine the contents of her closet at Mom's house, plus Mom's own closet.

She grabbed her key and emerged into the hotel hallway wearing jeans, flip flops, and a black mock-turtle neck for a stroll around downtown. She punched the down arrow. As the elevator arrived her phone rang. She looked down and saw Water Talon was calling.

"Hi Mr. Talon," she said. "Yes I have time to talk."

She turned and doubled back to her room, opened the door and settled in the chair next to the picture-window. After small talk mostly about the islands and the rebuilding in North Sound Bay, she launched into the recent events with Mathias. He listened quietly until she got into some details about the caves. When she talked about the map changing and lighting up, he became more animated.

"Did the map lines grow and change or actually move locations?" he asked.

Bev did not answer immediately, while watching the images in her mind's eye.

"Both occurred at different times," she said, "but the scale is so small on the map, and the caves are so big, and they go on forever, and the low-light in there makes the map hard to figure out."

Walter said nothing for half a minute, and the only sound was the crackling over the phone connection.

"When the lines move, I don't think about the direction. It's more of a knowing, an understanding," Bev said.

"You mean knowing where they're going to move? Or knowing what the treasure actually is?" he asked.

"No, not really," Bev whispered almost under her breath. The answer was bigger than his question. It was bigger than all his questions combined. A big-picture understanding of everything. It was an answer that Bev was not willing to try to explain, or to speculate on, or to guess at.

Bev felt her plate fill up with food for thought. Too many ideas at once, a buffet of information that was piled high to the ceiling. The conversation dribbled out slowly as she pulled back into herself, guarding all she knew and all she didn't know yet. Finally, they said their goodbyes.

THE NEXT DAY, Branson threw the convertible two-door into park at curbside pickup, jumped out onto the sidewalk to greet Bev, while grabbing her small carry-on. She abandoned her usual rule of dressing up for plane rides, and wore blue jeans with a slight split at one knee, a black silk button up blouse, and nondescript flats.

"You look great big Sis," he said. "Welcome to sunny California."

A smile crept across Bev's face as she looked out over the terminal building to a solid overcast mid-day sky. As they merged into traffic, Bev looked down and rolled her eyes at Branson's footwear. Boots made of soft leather that rippled around his ankles, over his shins and laced up to his knees. The heels were three inches high like western boots, but that's where the similarity ended. His shirt was a puffy silk, laying casually over his shoulders, with the hint of a lace collar. *Interesting get-up*, was what she thought, but said nothing. *After all, this is Branson.*

"I'm going to run you by my new museum, and then up to the foothills for lunch at the new Spanish cuisine cafe that I'm thinking about investing in," he said.

"Wait a minute, you have a museum?" Bev squealed.

"It's the coolest thing. Colonial Spanish artifacts and coins. I'm waiting for my life-size 16th Century horseman in full armor to be shipped from Minneapolis. It'll be the crown jewel of the exhibition," he exclaimed.

"Wait another minute. What about Minneapolis? They have Spanish horseman there?" Bev asked.

"It's a statue. They had an extra, so I bought it," he said.

"You bought it?"

Yep. I had some money sloshing around, because I resisted the urge to get rich on Bitcoin!" he said.

"Thanks, just rub it in," she replied, turned and looked out the window as they veered away from the airport toward downtown San Jose.

Bev's mind was rippling through all the events in Tennessee including the caves, treasure hunt, and of course the map. She was not paying attention as they took the ramp off the freeway into San Jose, past the wide, dreary streets populated with unremarkable buildings, dotted with random small restaurants and lunch counters. They flew by the City's signature institution, The Museum of Art, down a side street into an alley to a broken-concrete and gravel strewn parking lot.

Branson threw the car into park and looked up, "How do you like it?"

Bev raised her gaze to see a block building with a battered wooden staircase leading to a platform and a gray metal door.

"Like what? Where are we?"

"The museum. How do you like it?" he said.

Bev said nothing. She looked at Branson. Looked back at the whitewash peeling off the block building. Her lips parted as if she were going to talk, but could not think of a word to utter.

"This is the back of the building," he blurted. "The front looks better."

It was Bev's turn to say something. Her mouth opened slightly, but again only a bewildered breath passed through her lips. They climbed the rickety steps and entered the space. Branson flipped on the overhead florescent lights where a cluttered scene of scaffolding and old display cases littered the wood-plank floor. Branson led Bev to the front door that was flanked by large bay-widows.

"The windows are going away, and the front facade is turning into dark paneling. I found an old wooden twelve-foot-high door up in Sacramento. It's just right," he said.

"Just right?" Bev said.

"Mysterious. Think intriguing, secretive, cryptic. This will be out of the ordinary, touching people's senses, propelling them into a different world," Branson gleamed when he emitted the word "propelling."

"Did you buy it, or renting?" Bev asked.

"It's five blocks from the Museum of Art and City Center. Of course I bought it," he replied.

AFTER LUNCH, Branson's two-seater rolled down the tree-lined highway connecting San Jose to San Francisco, when the question that had been formulating in Bev's mind popped out.

"Are these Spanish colonial coins going to be a part of your museum collection?"

"Of course. Not only did those coins that mom and dad found make it all possible, but all that wealth robbed from Mexico and Central America and shipped to Spain are what made Spain a superpower back then," he said.

"Are there any special or let's say, magical coins?" Bev said.

Bev felt awkward as she spoke those words. *Magical coins? Magical ships floating around the Atlantic Ocean? Magical anything. Of course not, but she didn't know a better way to phrase an open-ended question meant to shake the tree that her brother was living in. Maybe some tidbit of obscurity that he nonchalantly ignored would fall out and shed some light on this stupid treasure map. Maybe even give her a good, solid reason to dump this whole endeavor.*

"What? Magical?" he said. "No nothing like that. Just plain-ole gold and silver," he said.

They pulled into their mother's house in Portola Valley around four in the afternoon. Bev dropped her bag on the front porch and rushed in to embrace her mom. She smelled chamomile in the air as she skipped back to the kitchen. *Finally home*, she thought, and as the screen door slammed behind her, Bev felt safe at last.

Then as if bursting through an invisible curtain, she felt something jumping up on her leg, yipping with exuberant squeals, "Who is this?" she screeched.

"Our new Beagle puppy," Alice said.

"What's his name?" Bev said.

"Buzzy. Buzzy the Beagle," Alice said. "Branson got him a couple of months ago."

"Does he live with Branson? Like does he take care of him and all that?" Bev asked.

Alice paused and let a smile creep onto her face, "Let's just say, this is Buzzy's summer home," Alice replied, "and summer is a flexible concept here."

Bev reached down and roughed up his coat while uttering goo-goo words interspersed with phrases like, Buzzy you're such a good boy. How did you get so cute, and on and on.

Buzzy finally settled at Bev's feet while she and her mom got comfortable at the breakfast bar with tea, and to catchup on all the details of the last few months.

Branson stayed a few minutes before leaving for a museum strategy meeting in Palo Alto. The Fairmont Gala started at five tomorrow and Branson would pick her up an hour before.

"Okay, Mom, what's with these boots Branson is wearing?" Bev asked.

"I thought your first question would be about the museum," she replied.

"Yeah, that too. So anyway, when did he get so weird?"

Alice paused just to let the whole concept of "weird" float through the kitchen and out the window.

"He likes to say it's being an entrepreneur. To me it's a shift toward eccentric. I feel like he's handling it, and hasn't shown too many signs of bizarre, yet," Alice postulated.

"What does Dad say about this sudden turn?" Bev said.

"So these days, your Dad is not a good judge of what bizarre is. He has talked to Branson about the conquistador outfit he's wearing a lot."

"And?"

"Branson insists he is differentiating himself...making himself a celebrity, like the little heiress, Paris Hilton, did a few years ago. You know, she was famous for doing nothing," Alice said, "and the Kardashians are Reality Royalty, whatever that means."

"It means a lot of people don't have anything important to think about; they have boring lives, and..."

Alice cut her off, "Bev, dear, let's be charitable. I view it as social norms that have broken down and been replaced by too much instant information. T.V. is probably the biggest culprit, but in the end, it probably drills down to phones and all the new technology. Too much, too fast," Alice said.

Bev took a sip of tea and it was her turn to let the words dissipate into thin air. Frantic innovation was a way of life for her, but she knew there was a slower pace only a few decades ago. She also knew there was no going back.

Alice's face relaxed as the tightness in her cheeks loosened. Her attention inched over to the center of the room and away from Bev, "Branson has too much time on his hands and he never uncovered a clear direction, at least nothing remotely conventional. Your father points out that history is packed with trust-fund offsprings that went into science, medicine, literature and made significant contributions to the world. Think about Darwin, for starters, he likes to point out," Alice said.

"I grant you that Branson is clever and smart, but not sure he's the next Darwin," Bev said.

"Darwin wasn't the next Darwin either," Alice replied, and they both laughed.

"It's not a good topic, though. He may be on the edge of eccentric," Alice said with a long sigh. "There, I said it."

"Like what?" Bev said.

"I didn't tell you that he showed up at Aunt Maureen's cookout looking like Captain Hook in a swashbuckling costume, a big hat with feathers, and giving out pieces of eight to the kids," Alice said. "He wore some sort of tights and boots with spurs, and what looked like a purple, embroidered curtain furled up over his shoulder."

"There's imagination for you. What did everybody else have on?"

"They wore shorts and flip flops. It wasn't a costume party. Branson just took it upon himself to be the weirdest person there," Alice said.

"Did the kids like it?"

"The little ones did, but I heard the older ones saying they hope they didn't turn out like that," Alice said. "I got him aside and asked him what he thought he was doing. He stayed in character like he was a pirate that just looted an English merchant ship. Get this, he handed me a gold doubloon and said, 'run along little girl.'" Alice said.

"Did you slap him, Mom?"

"This is way beyond slapping," Alice said. "Besides, I was afraid I'd dislodge the glued-on mustache," she managed a chuckle, which got no acknowledgment from Bev.

"The last thing I need right now is more stress, but would it help if I talked to him and take his temperature, so to speak?" Bev asked.

"I don't have an answer to that or any of this stuff with your brother," Alice said.

"Mom?" Bev blurted. "Don't people grow out of this kind of stuff?"

Bev noticed a single tear rolling over her mother's cheek. Alice stood up, went to the sink to rustle some dishes around, before cautiously making her way back to the breakfast bar.

Buzzy strolled into the room brushing against Bev's leg, who hopped off her chair and started cooing and rubbing him to his delight.

CHAPTER
EIGHTEEN

The Fairmont Hotel lobby buzzed with activity and the ballroom was decorated to the nines. Bev wore a black cocktail dress that she dug out of her mother's closet, black low-heeled pumps, and a string of white pearls. Black usually looked stunning on her, flattering her bronze complexion and coal-black hair. This night was no exception. She let the doorman help her from the car and walked in. Her severe trepidation, slowly morphed into mild bewilderment as she entered the hotel. Not looking over at Branson, she attempted to ignore her brother; the spectacle that was her date for the evening.

The lace-up knee-high boots were gone, way too casual, and were replaced by black tights with a distinctive sheen. A short apron/skirt made of thin metal strips hung from his waist. From the waist up, an olive-brown light-weight metal chemise laid over his shoulders, topped off with white cotton ruffles around his neck. Bev told him that the helmet had to stay in the car or she was going home.

Eccentric! Not even! Bizarre, Depraved, that's closer, but still won't describe the way I'm feeling about this, Bev thought. *I'll pretend I just happen to be standing next to him, but I don't know him, just random chance, but it'll never fly. I'm busted. The weirdest brother in San Francisco...and that's really saying something.*

All eyes turned to Branson as the revolving door shuffled them into the lobby and revealed the only Spanish Conquistador in the room, or maybe anywhere outside Spain, fully ready for battle. *Here we go,* she thought, *just smile and pretend nothing is wrong. We got the dates mixed up and thought it was a costume party. Never work,* she thought.

I am totally sure this is the biggest fake smile in the history of the world that I'm wearing to cover up my total unraveling, she thought.

Then, stranger-than-strange. A well-appointed young man in a black suite made a point to cross the room and walk up to Branson.

"Hey Branson. Good to see you. I heard you were attending tonight. You look great and by the way, I like the tights. Giving the boots a rest, I see," he said.

Bev felt light-headed, took a couple of steps backward to a chair and grabbed its back to steady herself. Then she watched a stranger walk over to Branson to comment, "Nice going. Not sure what you're doing with this, but I like the vibe," he said.

A thirty-something woman with high heels, long brown hair, and dressed to kill, stepped up and said, "Very handsome." She put a calling card in his hand, and as she turned to walk away, she stopped in front of Bev. She was practically starring with a familiarity that made Bev think they must have met before.

Then she spoke with a causal, nonchalant air, "I can see you shivering in a dark, cold room, no not a room, a cave," she paused while diverting her stare to the space around Bev. "I see fear and confidence wrapped up together," she continued, "You're in big danger following this map-thing," she said while pausing for a breath. "Oh wow, there is even bigger danger in not pursuing it. It's really clear. What a cool adventure. I'd wish you good luck, but it won't make any difference." As she pivoted and slowly walked away, Bev heard her mutter under her breath, "Cool Beans."

"Who the heck was that," Bev asked.

"I have no idea. Never seen her before," Branson replied.

"Well, what does her card say?"

Without looking at it, he handed the card to Bev. She held it up and starred at the writing. "Rachel, 415-Cool Bns."

"It says Rachel and a phone number. I think it says 'cool beans.'"

After a few seconds, Bev said, "She was telling me stuff that she shouldn't know. I mean stuff in Tennessee that is way out in the ether and out of her reality, like dream stuff, like she was reading my mind.

"Probably one of these mystic whacko-psychics, well, you know," he said.

"You sound like this is normal stuff. Mystic whackos?"

"Where do you think we are, Hoboken? This is San Francisco. Whacky is cool here."

Bev took another look at the Conquistador standing next to her and thought, *I'm starting to get dizzy.*

LATER AFTER SITTING down to dinner, Bev watched as Branson tried to butter a piece of bread. The elbows in the armor had built-in flexibility, but more for swinging a sword or reining in a stallion in the heat of battle. This battle with a butter knife was new territory, and he was losing.

Bev leaned over to Branson not even attempting to disguise her giggling and said, "I think you're supposed to eat before you arrive in that getup."

She reached for her wine glass exuberantly, and drained it. Branson reached into his top-breast pocket, pulled out a coin, and handed the gold doubloon to Bev.

She smirked and said, "Thanks, your Royal Highness."

Branson fielded that comment by looking across the room with a blank, detached expression. Then looked at Bev.

"This one has great power. It's the doubloon of magic powers. The power is for you, my Big Sis."

Branson greeted another well-wisher while Bev clutched the coin and sat back in her chair, feeling helpless.

WHEN BEV SETTLED into the non-stop flight to Nashville, she had her earphones clamped over her head. *Home is home after all,* she thought, *but I'm not sure I want to fit into those old patterns. Mom is nurturing, not sure I need nurture. Dad is tripping on delusions of grandeur, and Branson is an alien having been dropped off in the penal colony of Earth, a hundred light years from the mother planet.*

Bev looked out the window at thirty thousand feet and felt a sadness creep in, a sorry for myself vibe, a pity party for one. She felt a tear begin to well up in her eyes. *How can I fit into that crazy California scene,* she thought. *I need stability.*

Like a lightning bolt piercing the billowing cumulus cloud bank surrounding the 737 Luxury Liner, it struck her. The tears poised to roll down her cheeks and confirm her life predicament evaporated, replaced first by a simmering smile, then a chuckle and without warning a full out laugh. Heads turned as this unprovoked outburst startled the nearby passengers.

You're on a plane escaping the chaos of family skeletons and heading to the stability of a map that moves and changes at will, a hunt for treasure of unknown value in an ancient cave system that's hundreds of miles long, a distant cousin that may be a closet madman, and a new romance with a country-boy lawyer that you think is going to save your life. Yep that's stability, all right, she thought.

Bev could feel those looking at her saying, *What's so funny. I want a good laugh too. You look like a nice girl, spill the beans, come on, no holding out.*

CHAPTER
NINETEEN

Price helped lift Bev's left foot into the stirrup of the western saddle.

"Grab the horn and pull up, I'll give you a shove," he said.

Bev spent a lot of time in the ring as a teenager learning to cantor and trot, but it was always on an English saddle. She looked up to the horse's back and eyed the saddle horn, grabbed it and hoisted herself up. The horse shifted its weight from one back leg to the other, but otherwise stayed steady.

"Good. Grab the reins and keep her still," Price said.

Price then took the reins of his sorrel-colored mare and pulled himself up onto the saddle. He looked over at Bev, sitting straight and steady, holding the reins of the black and white, paint-colored horse. Her name was Janey-Ray and he chose her for Bev, not because she had the most unique markings, but because she was calm and reliable.

"Let's go. Follow me through the gate and we'll head to that big open field and then down to the woods. There's a trail through the trees that's my favorite," Price said.

Price gave his horse a slight nudge with his heels moving to a trot. Janey-Ray followed instantly. Price turned, looked over his shoulder to see Bev riding like a champ. He eased the reins and let his heels punch again, taking him to a cantor. Bev lifted herself slightly off the saddle and slid into the rhythm.

The field was wide open and the grass was only knee-deep. Price knew that "wide-open" was a frame of reference, but not an open invitation to go anywhere. The cave network that crisscrossed underneath the land frequently caused sinkholes to appear that could break a horse's leg and toss its rider to the ground.

As a kid in these fields, Price was at a full run when suddenly a five-foot wide sinkhole appeared. His horse could not avoid it and drove both front legs into the front edge of the pit. As her knees bent and her legs folded back, Price was laid gently on the grass, but before he could move, the mare's body collapsed on his legs. He and the horse laid still, as both horse and rider were stunned.

Price turned and shook his head trying to get a handle on the situation. The mare lifted up and tried to get to her feet, but fell back. On the second try, she made it to all fours, gave a shake and with both saddle and bridle took off in a slow trot to the barn. Price got to his feet and started walking slowly back, achy and shaken but okay. As he walked through the open field he felt a little embarrassed and knew he'd catch grief from the farm hands at the barn. *What the heck,* he thought, *they've all walked back to the barn before.* He began thinking about the feeling of freedom he felt riding in that field with just him, his horse and the wind. In the vein of, 'mistakes are the only way you learn,' he approached the barn with the recognition that freedom is not always free. Freedom has a cost. He noted in his mind to look for sinkholes from now on.

Bev was soaking up the view of the landscape of Southern country. It made the dry, brown hills of California look like a desert. The view was lush-green from the pastures to the timberline. They settled into a slow pace with the horses at a smooth walk through the mostly flat forest trails. Then the trail turned left and up a steep hill. The horses were ready and instantly dug into low gear as they trudged to the top. The trees parted and Bev saw a wide-open knoll overlooking the rolling hills. From there she saw cornfields, cattle grazing, ponds and streams. She smiled and took a deep breath. *Okay,* she thought, *not home but not bad.*

Price looked out over the landscape that he knew so well. He dismounted, tied the reins to a branch, and walked over to Bev.

"Can I help you down, Lady Godiva?" he quipped.

They settled on a grassy spot opening a pack of cashews to snack on.

"I know I don't need to tell you, but this is so gorgeous," Bev said.

"My mom inherited those four hundred acres on the left down in the valley. It's been in the family for generations. I lease the farmland and grazing area to a neighbor. It's not worth a fortune or anything. The big money would be in developing it, but it's too far from town," Price said as he took a breath. "I don't know what I'd do with that kind of money anyway."

Bev felt slightly faint, in some sort of time warp, and thought she should respond, but far from being blank, her mind was racing. Silicon Valley was not a place you heard someone, or anyone, say, "I don't know what I'd do with that kind of money."

She tumbled into a blackhole of childhood thoughts: *Dad, Branson, Mom, Grandpa Richard. Was it all about the money? The coins? The treasure hunt?* She didn't know the answers. She sat and was speechless. Time passed until she noticed Price stretched out facing the sky but with closed eyes. In a single stealth motion, she leaned over and gently put her lips on his. He reached behind her head, cradle it, as they rolled over in the grass.

After a while Bev sat up and Price said, "Okay tell me about this trip to San Francisco?"

"I can tell you that my brother is a certified nut-case, and he gets it from my father, and my mother is doing her normal thing, and everybody else is trying to get rich," Bev said.

"That's a mouthful. What normal things does she do?" Price asked.

"My mother gardens and fools with all the family machinations. And... and...Well, my mother is a psychic, although she keeps it low key," Bev's voice trailed off.

"Really?" Price said.

"Yeah, there's the California Paranormal thing in Palo Alto. She keeps me out of it, mostly."

Bev looked away and Price looked back out over the land.

"Price, do you know anything about this map Mathias has? Or, the caves he's talking about?" Bev asked.

Price lifted his arm pointing out over the landscape below, "Look down there on those fields. If the grass weren't high, you'd see pock-marks all over them from the limestone sinkholes. There are caves everywhere. Is there something valuable hidden in them? Sure there is. Just like there is an Easter Bunny," he said. "As far as the map goes, my step-dad keeps all that stuff to himself, except one day he was lost in thought and blurted out a bunch of random details about it," he said.

"What do you think about it all?" she asked.

"I think it's like buying a lottery ticket on Mars. No chance. He doesn't even know what he's looking for," he said. "I know all about the map. It sits on the table and turns Mathias into a lunatic who's harder and harder to get along with," he said.

Price's next words formed in his mind, but never made it to his lips. Sitting tight and letting Bev vent this map stuff was the best move right now. He knew there was no counter argument for the spirit or psychic stuff.

Price dated Melissa in college. Met her in the student grill his sophomore year. It was intriguing when she tossed three pennies down six times and then read a passage from the ancient Chinese Book of Changes, *The I Ching*. Insights into life? Okay, deep thoughts, but Price wasn't buying it. Melissa consulted the Tarot Cards before each date. He wasn't buying it. One night Price showed up for a date and read a note on the door, *Hi Price, I'm gone to Boulder. Have a nice life.*

He didn't think that Bev was going to Boulder, and he saw nothing that showed Bev was another Melissa, so he just listened. Bev was a business major and knew nothing about Chinese mysticism, or Tarot Cards. She didn't know much about this map other than she thinks the lines move. *That'll work its way out,* he thought.

The sun was low in the western sky when they mounted up. Price led the way around the wooded trail they had come up, and down the opposite side, until they reached the open field. It looked like about four in the afternoon and Price thought a nice stroll through the grassy field would be just fine. He told Bev his sinkhole story so she'd grasp the caution that he learned the hard way.

Riding side-by-side there was little talk, just riding. Price pulled ahead for a few minutes. Bev gave Janey-Ray a slight nudge to catch up, and as she did, her horse stopped suddenly and without warning reared up on her back legs. She came down with her front hoofs lashing out at a spot on the grass. That's when Bev got a good look at the rattle snake coiling for a strike. Panic struck Bev, but she could do nothing. The snake uncoiled and lurched for Janey-Ray's knee, but missed and fell flat on the grass, unprotected. Then two hoofs pounded against the ground, one hit the middle section of the snake at the same time the other landed on its head, pulverizing it.

It happened in seconds and the only thing Price saw was Janey-Ray on two back legs. He tried to turn around but he was too late. Janey-Ray took off toward the barn in a full-out run. Bev dropped the reins in the commotion and was holding on to the saddle horn. They were on a straight line to the barn, but both stirrups slid off her feet, and finally the shaking dislodged Bev from the saddle and she slid off the back. She hit on her bottom and rolled sideways avoiding whiplash to her neck. By the time Price arrived, she was standing but unsure on her feet. He gently helped her sit back down, moving slowly giving her time to settle.

When they got to the barn, two farm hands were standing out near the fence waiting. They saw Janey-Ray arrive and knew there was trouble. Price sat in the saddle while they helped Bev off the back of the horse. No obvious broken bones, but Price loaded her in the back seat of the farm pickup and headed to the emergency room anyway.

BRANSON THOUGHT BETTER than to wear a conquistador costume to the hospital. For one thing, it would be distracting and second, for Christ's sake, this was Tennessee. The last time he was here was as a ten-year old, and he wore shorts and a tee shirt. Branson worked at being eccentric but he wasn't a nihilist. At least he didn't think so. Concurrence on this topic among his acquaintances in California was not a hundred percent, however.

He breezed right by Price Davis as he rounded the corner of the waiting area and into Bev's room. It was four in the afternoon and visiting hours just ended.

"Okay big sis, where does it hurt and where is this cowboy that got you into this mess?" Branson blurted.

"Hi Branson, there's a hairline fracture in my forearm and signs of a concussion. My shoulder is slightly dislocated and sore, but could have been worse," Bev said.

"Slightly dislocated? What does that mean?" he said.

"It means maybe it's more than slight, so with this concussion thing, they are keeping me here for a couple of days. I managed to insist on a chiropractor. We'll see him in about half an hour," she said.

"Should I tear this cowboy to shreds with my bear hands for this?" he said with a grimace on his face.

"For one thing, he's not a cowboy. And second, you'll have trouble tearing anything apart with those school-boy hands of yours," Bev paused. "Price grew up in public school, and hauled hay in the summer...quick, savvy, and strong...way out of your league."

"What does hauling hay mean?"

"It means lifting seventy-five-pound bales from the ground onto a moving truck for eight or ten hours a day," she said.

"And the crack about public school?"

"While Price was hauling hay, you were probably knitting sweaters," she laughed out loud.

Branson let that snarky comment sink to the floor by its own weight. He seemed glad that his sister still had her wit and humor, even at his expense.

"Does Mom know you're here?" Bev asked.

"I called her from the plane. She's ready to come out if you need her," he said.

"Let's call her after this next adjustment. Did you fly private?" she said.

"They had a plane leaving San Francisco to Birmingham, and I was able to get to the airport in forty-five minutes to hitch a ride," he replied.

Bev's eyes diverted as Price walked through the door with the chiropractor.

"Price, I want you to meet my brother, Branson," Bev said. "He dropped by for a free meal," she giggled to everyone's approval.

After introductions, Bev told them to go out in the hall and get acquainted while the chiropractor worked on her.

The two young men walked out to the waiting room, squared off slightly and then both sat down. There was a silence, not for minutes, but for a few seconds before Branson spoke.

"How did the doctors let a chiropractor in here? Come on, doctors are afraid of those guys."

"Yeah well, there's a lot of new therapies doctors are afraid of," Price said. "Bev took the reins and insisted on getting adjustments."

"I had my first adjustment at ten years old. It was normal at our house," Branson said.

Price took a deep breath, "She got a good shakin' up but she'll be okay."

Price told the story of the snake and the gallop to the barn as they settled in and waited.

MATHIAS WHIPPED into the underground parking, paying little attention to his surroundings. His truck straddled the lines of two spaces. In one continuous motion, he shoved it into park and grabbed the map. He was frantic and focused on the map, the treasure, the urgency. If Bev were disabled, he would have no possibility of following the map and finding the treasure.

He didn't know what happened, but feared the worst. Price sent him a text and it merely said, "Bev slid off Janey-Ray at a full gallop. She's in the hospital." Calling the small hospital near the farm, he got her room number. He punched the elevator button, but when the doors failed to immediately open, he went to the stairs and leaped up two steps at a time until he reached the fourth floor. He wiped the droplets of sweat off his forehead with his shirtsleeve, and entered the corridor leading to room 443.

In the waiting area, Price had his back to the corridor and although Branson saw Mathias streak by, Price didn't notice his step-father at first, but flinched slightly as he caught Mathias, out of the corner of his eye, duck into Bev's room. Branson continued telling Price about his grandfather and the treasure hunt and mystery his dad and mom solved. He was rolling into a description of the Spanish coins, and although Price was nodding his head like he was paying attention, he was not.

Price turned his head to see the empty doorway with no movement in or out. As he took a first step in that direction, he said, "Let's see how it's going in there."

Branson started to say, 'what's the rush,' but Price was already at the doorway and out of earshot.

Bev was contorted with her right hand reaching around to hold her left shoulder and the chiropractor was holding both with a gentle knee touching her lower back and pulling slightly. Price noticed Mathias was standing to the side and cautiously making small talk with Bev. Price knew Mathias well and he could see the slight smile and good humor were made up and not genuine. He shook his head imperceptibly. Then he noticed a small table behind Mathias with a large scroll laying on it. *Is that the map?* he thought.

"There, I got the movement in that shoulder I'm looking for," the chiropractor said. "It'll require some rest, but right now I want you to keep your back straight and take a lap around the fourth floor. Being upright will help this shoulder settle in," he paused. "If you don't feel pain from walking, you can take the elevator down to the cafeteria. Just stay standing. Come back to the room when you get tired."

Uncharacteristically, Mathias jumped up and insisted that he would help Bev on this walk. They slowly started out of the room with Mathias holding Bev's waist to keep her stable.

After their round trip to the cafeteria, she and Mathias walked back into the room, Bev read the note on her pillow out loud, "I've taken Branson for a quick meal to Ma's Place for some catfish. We'll be back shortly. Price."

Mathias smiled with a sigh of relief. This would give him time alone with Bev and the map.

"Looks like you're going to be okay," he said. "I was worried your mother would kill me if I let something happen to you down here."

"Thanks cousin," she replied. "She wouldn't blame you for anything. She knows I'm a big girl and can handle myself," ...*at least I think she does*, she thought to herself.

"I've been down to the cave recently and there are some interesting new twists," he said. There was urgency in his delivery, because he knew the boys would be back soon.

"Really," she replied halfheartedly.

"Yes, here I'll show you," he said as he turned and reached for the map, but his eyes stared at an empty tabletop. A flash of fear engulfed him for a split-second as he stooped to look on the floor and behind the table.

"Oh the map, I guess somebody moved it," he whispered. "Let's see where it can be?"

Mathias talked with a kind of "happy" twist in his voice. A little too happy for Bev. He had been cordial and friendly in the short time she had been in Tennessee, but this felt patronizing, a little bit too cute. She felt cautious as she crawled under the bedsheet and was happy to not be looking at any map, especially that one. Mathias drilled into every corner and closet and turned up nothing.

"I'll check with the staff," he said. "Be right back."

He could find no sign of the map. He flew down the steps to the garage and tore open the passenger door of his truck. No map. He looked under the truck. Traced his steps back up the stairs. Took half an hour looking into every corner of the 4th floor. He walked into private offices, interrupting meetings, checking drawers. No map. Wiping the beads of sweat from his face with his sleeve, he walked into Bev's room.

Branson looked up from his seat in the chair and Price gave a nod, but kept talking to Bev.

"Seems like I've misplaced something," Mathias said. "You guys see a scrolled-up tube anywhere?"

"I didn't. How about you Branson?" Price said.

"No nothing like that."

THE NEXT MORNING, Buzzy weaved his way through the revolving door of the hospital. He glided into the lobby like a trained investigator, smooth, confident, and in control. Branson followed his canine companion. His conquistador persona was astutely left hanging in the hotel closet, with the exception of the knee-high boots laced up the front. He knew he was in the country where people practiced the art of "mind your own business." If the few people he passed noticed the boots, they were "minding their..." well, you know.

Buzzy was bluntly turned away at a hospital in Los Angeles just last week when Branson was visiting, but today he inched into the elevator and headed to the 4th floor. Bev raised her eyes the minute he pranced into her room. A stranger might think that Buzzy and Bev were tight-as-ticks, but the truth was, Buzzy was tight with everybody he met. After greeting Bev, he started his investigation of the room in the corners, and worked his way across the entire room.

"Wow, he stays busy," Bev said.

"Beagles do that," Branson said. "They smell hundreds of times better than we do."

Bev sat up and put her hand down below the bed. Buzzy was there in a heart-beat with a tongue bath for her.

Around eleven the discharge papers arrived and Branson along with Buzzy walked Bev to a waiting Ford SUV, and on to Price's condominium on West End Avenue.

CHAPTER
TWENTY

Bev rose from bed and walked through the short hallway into the living area of Price's small bungalow in Nashville. It was small but had three bedrooms, and Price insisted that Bev and Branson stay there while things settled. Price popped up from his chair with a gesture toward her, while Branson merely turned his head acknowledging her. Price was giving her a bit of the China-doll treatment...fragile, broken, needy. Branson acted like it was his sister who could take a fall and shake it off. He'd seen her do it all his life. When he was a whiny little brother, Bev taught him to toughen up. He was confident that Bev could manage this. Price was anything but confident, because he was in the throes of falling in love.

"The coffee's on the counter," Branson pointed.

Price took a step toward the kitchen, but Bev held her hand up to stop him, and then took the few steps to the coffee pot.

"We've got skydiving tomorrow at eight, or we could make it ten-thirty," Branson said.

"Very funny, Jimmy," Bev said.

"Jimmy?" Price asked.

"Jimmy Kimmel," she said. "Branson's being Mister Funny."

Buzzy moved from Branson over to Bev offering her a few licks on the hand as she sat down.

"I talked to Mom last night," Bev said. "I told her there was no need to fly out here, and I'd swing out there in a few days."

Price dropped his head ever so slightly and his gaze moved down when hearing this disappointing news.

"What's your plan?" Bev said looking at Branson.

"No plan at the moment," he replied. "Buzzy and I have noticed there is a lack of supervision here, so we may hang around for a while."

Price looked over to Bev as she gave a nonchalant eye-roll. Buzzy settled in at Bev's feet.

"Tell me about my cousin Mathias," Branson said.

"My Mom married him when I was eleven," Price said.

"So he raised you?"

"Yeah, he stepped in after my dad died. He never had any kids and I think he liked having an excuse to go to Little League and help me with homework," Price said. "He was a construction engineer and worked a lot in Florida. Before Mom died, he cut back and was home more, but things kind of started changing and I'm not sure what happened. His interest in maps just came out of the blue. Mom used to say, 'it's that silly old map.' But that's all I knew.

"What about this map?" Branson said. "Is this thing for real?"

Bev sat back in her chair and lowered her gaze. Even to her brother, her weird brother, she didn't know how to explain the map...the lines moving...the points lighting up...the sensitivity she felt. The things she understood about the map that she had no words for. She was confused, but as contradictory as it seemed, she felt a sense of certainty about it all, an uneasy certainty.

"I don't know what 'for real' means, but it is real," Price said.

He inched his way out of the chair and over to the sliding glass door. Reaching behind the curtain, his hand emerged with a scrolled tube tightly bound by two rubber bands. Bev looked up and gasped.

"What is that doing here?" she said.

It was almost an accusation, but Price put on his lawyer hat and let the comment bounce off.

"Mathias has been a mess since he got this map and it is past time to put a stop to it," he said. "Out of sight out of mind, is my theory."

This 'out of sight' theory fell on deaf ears for Bev, because it was in plain sight in front of her. She felt a safe distance as long as Mathias had the map...a take-it-or-leave-it attitude. The power of the map was strong and these men had no idea what kind of fire they were playing with.

"Great. Let's take a look at the famous map," Branson said.

Price cleared the center-piece from the table and rolled out the map, weighting down the four corners. The map covered the table top as Branson pulled the chairs away to make room to stand. He began pointing out symbols of water, mountains, and other squiggles that were common in treasure maps. Price had seen the map on a few occasions, but paid little attention to it. Branson pointed to images on the upper right.

"These are kind of hard to make out, but look like they could be part of a coat-of-arms that ruling regimes used all over the world. It reminds me of the Spanish symbols on the coins," he said. "I don't want to jump-the-gun, but look at the top of that shield. It looks like the unique symbol used in the reign of Phillip V, the Spanish King around the 1730-time frame. I can't make it out exactly because of these odd lines running across it. Never seen those kinds of lines."

Bev sat, transfixed and silent. She fought off her first instinct to blurt out the meaning of the 'odd lines'. She was struggling to stay neutral as they investigated the map. Bev knew without looking that those lines were the caves. At the same time, she felt a queasy feeling and was certain that the directions were morphing and moving, and equally confident that the boys were not seeing the changes. She felt scared and alone. Then the words of Grandpa came to her, *you have bigger fish to fry*. Still petrified and unwilling to move, the words rang again in her ear, *bigger fish to fry*.

She finally rose from the chair and stood in front of the table. She didn't look at the map, but simply said, "Let's go down in the caves tomorrow."

BRANSON OPENED the door of his rental car and glanced at his watch, 9:35. His boots were spanking-new from the Army-Navy store and while functional, did not match the black tights, burgundy ruffled-shirt, warrior skirt made of strips of aluminum draped from his waist, and topping it off with a three-cornered hat and a white peacock feather protruding out the back. He shut the car door and in the outside mirror, caught a glimpse of himself as this make-shift conquistador as he walked by.

Price heard the knock and opened the front door. To Branson's surprise, he said nothing. Bev apprised him of her brother's eccentricities first thing that morning. "What's a treasure hunt without a good conquistador?" he reasoned.

Bev had explained the directions to the cave entrance from her last visit with Mathias as best as she remembered. They had been riding about half an hour when Bev noticed that the fields and landscape didn't seem familiar to her.

"Is this the right way?" she said to Price.

"It is the right way, but not your cave. It's a hidden entrance that only a few people know about. I thought we'd start there," he said.

She instantly felt like saying, *no the map is leading the other way*. But she stayed silent, not wanting to tip her hand and have to explain the secrets of the map.

Why not, she thought with a tinge of guilt. *These guys are on my side.*

The car was silent for half a minute, which seemed like an eternity. *It's a long way from a paper map to the ethereal reality of the strange energy going on. Spoon feed the info, slowly so they will be able to grasp it*, she thought.

"Cool. Tell us about this secret entrance," Bev said.

"A kid I grew up with took me there. His big brother knew about it. It floods sometimes in the spring and the county gated it off after some kid drowned. There are some windy passages and some really old drawings on the walls," Price said.

Bev got the picture that Price was satisfying the cave itch by going sightseeing. She settled back and put the map out of her mind, for now.

The truck left the dirt road and the bumps made it feel like they were tumbling down a steep hill, finally reaching flat ground. Price navigated his way through a rain-soaked scruffy field and into a forest of mostly sapling trees. He made his own road through the trees for only a few hundred yards until he stopped the engine.

"We're here. Let's go," he said.

Branson was uncharacteristically silent as they followed Price on foot to a nondescript hill covered in green brush. As they stopped, Buzzy made a beeline to the edge of the foliage and disappeared under the branches.

"What's this," said the conquistador.

"Come on, follow me Ferdinand," Price said with a smirk eliciting a giggle from Bev.

They pushed past the bushes and like magic walked into an opening about six feet high.

"Okay Columbus, looks like we have ourselves a cave," Branson said directing his comment to Price. That got another giggle from Bev.

Thoughts of the map started to melt away and Bev was glad of it.

With some daylight still illuminating the way into the cave entrance, they came across a gate with a giant padlock clamping it to an iron fence. Price stuck his hand behind the sign that read, KEEP OUT. CLOSED TO THE PUBLIC. As his hand pulled back, the sign dropped to the dirt exposing a three-foot wide gap in the gate.

"How did you know that was there?" Bev asked.

He looked at her nonchalantly and said, "I know things. Just leave it at that."

They crawled through the gate, fired up flashlights and began walking on a dry, sand path with Buzzy in the lead. A dip in the path took them through a short stretch of wet sand and clay. The ceiling dipped to around five feet causing Branson to pull his feathered hat off. Then without a word, Price veered off to the left taking a small narrow passage. Bev wanted a bit of explanation as to why they abandoned the main corridor before she admitted to herself that she was lost either way, so she might as well follow the leader. Branson taking up the rear, followed Bev, while Buzzy again was the advance scout. Then Price stopped and waited as they all caught up.

"Turn off your flashlight on the count of three," Price said. "One, two, three."

The silence was as deafening as the darkness was black. Not dark, mind you, but BLACK. Any thoughts about a dark winter night in deep cloud-cover and no-moon-visible kind of black was stripped from their minds. This was scary-black. Buzzy gave a yelp, Branson stayed silent swallowing a lump in his throat, and Bev muttered, "Price?"

Price flicked his light back on and gave a muffled chuckle, "Okay, follow me."

After a few minutes, he stopped again then pointed his light to the ceiling. Bev looked up to see a forty-foot ceiling covered partially in a pearly-white gleam. She pointed her light ahead and illuminated a floor-to-ceiling pillar. As she moved her light, pillar after pillar appeared, stalactites meeting stalagmites throughout this giant cavern.

Buzzy slowed his investigations and stood next to Branson. Price found a seat on a bulging limestone outcropping giving time for the others to fill their eye with the wonders of this cave. That is exactly what Bev was doing. The map didn't cross her mind, nor did feelings or thoughts of the treasure hunt. She stood and soaked up the spectacle all around her.

Price stood up slowly and made his way to a nearby corner of the cave. He shined his flashlight on the wall, contemplated it for a half minute and then called to the others. Buzzy arrived first, and then Bev and Branson inched their way to stand facing the wall.

Bev stared and then said, "Are those pictures carved or painted on the wall? They almost look scratched into the rock."

"They're called petroglyphs, and they may be over four thousand years old. People, animals...that's what they drew then," Price said.

"Did they mean something? I mean religious or spiritual or fertility gods or something like that?" Branson said.

"These scratched-on ones are thought to be just pictures with no real meaning," Price replied. "But over thousands of years some of the later drawings used color from charcoal and colored clay, and some people interpret those as some sort of ritual images. I think they're called pictographs."

"Sounds like a lot of guess-work with this stuff," Branson said.

Bev found herself staring at the petroglyphs, and as she did, she felt a sensation, almost a presence in the room. This feeling floated around her and started to move deeper, when she suddenly lifted her chin, made a deep sound clearing her throat, and walked over to stand by Price. *Shake it off. Going spacey is the last thing you need right now*, she thought.

CHAPTER
TWENTY-ONE

Alice looked up from her folding chair in the small annex on the second floor of the California Paranormal Research Institute in Palo Alto. She was sitting in meditation with her regular Thursday morning group. It was an offshoot of classes from the clairvoyant teaching program. She took a class or two before Grandpa Richard died and before he sent them on the treasure hunt that changed everybody's life. The group formed while she and Andrew were chasing pieces of eight and gold doubloons down in the islands. Winning that fortune only started the problems in the family, so she looked for places to be calm and start to grow past it all when she drifted back into the group.

"Hi everybody, I'm Elizabeth, as you all know, and I'm the session leader today. Close your eyes. See your cosmic energy flow through you from the top of your head through your seventh chakra. Feel it nudge out the gray energy and now replace it with gold. Feel your total essence all through your body," she said. "Keri will be our control person and will keep the energy clear for us."

After a few minutes of silence, Elizabeth said, "Alice, I see an impasse around your third chakra. It looks like there are problems with Bev or Branson."

Alice straightened her back in the chair and said, "Bev fell off a horse in Tennessee and she's in the hospital."

"I don't see any lasting problems for her...her energy looks positive," Elizabeth went on. "I see Branson's energy, but there's somebody else that's encroaching on Bev's space. It doesn't look great."

"That's her new boyfriend, Price. He's a country music singing-lawyer. She's head-over-heels," Alice said.

"Yes I see that, but this is a different person. This energy looks kind of scary," Elizabeth said.

"Is his name Mathias?" Alice asked. "I've seen some odd things around my cousin, Mathias, lately."

"Yes, looks like it. He's more than scary!" Keri said. "This guy is evil. I hate to use that word, but I can really see it. Bev is strong, but maybe not strong enough for this Mathias character."

"There's another energy here. It's all over Mathias but it's not his. This stuff is coming up from the earth's core. It's dangerous; it's ugly," Elizabeth said. "I hear screams and feel pain, ugly. I'm feeling it."

Just then the room felt dark. The mood slumped and the whole group lost their grounding. Keri called in her spirit master, Zachary, who had helped her clear dark energy in the past. Alice could see the image of Zachary standing next to Keri, but rather than reacting, he stood silent and appeared helpless in the face of this darkest spirit. Fear engulfed the room and Alice felt the entire building shaking. Opening her eyes, she could see the curtains hanging still and the furniture flat on the floor. No shaking there. All were holding the sides of their chairs...they all sensed the shakes anyway. A half-minute passed that felt like an hour, as the darkness ebbed and slowly retreated. The group began opening their eyes.

Elizabeth cleared her throat and in a quiet, calm voice said in a whisper, "Looks like we have some work to do."

A FEW DAYS LATER, Bev ran into the bedroom, grabbed her phone and punched the green button to answer on the fourth ring without looking at caller ID. It was around 11:00 in the morning and she expected the call would be from one of a short list of people. Settling into Price's farm house in the country, she had resisted her mother's insistence to fly back to California. Alice mentioned something about a disturbing meeting with her group, but without being specific. Bev decided to stay in Nashville. Price had driven Branson and Buzzy to the airport a few days earlier to jump a Lear Jet to the coast.

Maybe this call would be Mathias wanting to talk about the map...or find where the map is? She had never been good at lying and always felt that anyone or even everyone could see any lie she was telling. So, it terrified her to fib. As usual, she let this feeling move into her very bones and was apprehensive.

"Hello," she gave a guarded salutation.

"Hi Bev, I'm glad to get hold of you. It's been a while and I'm curious, how things are going?"

"I'm not sure I know who this is...unless. Are you Walter? Walter Talon?"

"Right you are, Miss Bev Dahl, granddaughter of the treasure-Meister, Richard Dennison," Walter said. "I feel like I shouldn't be prying, but I'm wondering about the map and if it's taken you on any adventures?"

"Nice of you to call. My latest adventure is falling off a galloping mare in a hay field in Tennessee," Bev said.

Walter felt his throat tense up. He knew it was his turn to speak, but he stayed quiet and owned his silence. He expected her to be cavorting around California with some weirdo map stories for her friends, and living the rich-girl lifestyle. "In Tennessee" meant the map may have caught her up in that crazy spell that he barely escaped. She had all the gold and silver coins she could want. It wasn't the riches that attracted her.

With caution, Walter began, "Are you a country music fan?"

"It's rubbing off on me. Never knew much about it, other than a few hit songs that made it to the pop charts."

"Country songs can paint a picture and tell a story. At least the good ones can. I like that one, *Nickel Beer*. Really kind of funny, but tells a true-life story," he said.

He paused and there was a silence, as Bev walked through the kitchen and out to the screen porch. She sat in a wicker chair and lifted her feet to rest on the ottoman.

"Well Walter, I'm staying in the country outside Nashville, while I recover from the fall. It's not California and thank goodness it's not New York."

"Is the New York gig over for good.?" he said.

"Yes, for good."

"And that boy up there?"

"For good," she said with some emphasis. As she did, a slight feeling of guilt snuck in and erased the smirk that had formed on her face. *It's not Darien's fault. He's doing what he went there to do. He has to make his way,* she thought. *I need to find myself, but he is going the wrong way for me.*

Walter opened his mouth to speak, but instead lifted his eyes to look out over the green pasture mowed short by hungry cattle on his Georgia farm. He had a brain full of questions like you do when you're gossiping about an old enemy, hoping to hear the dirty war stories. But the curiosity had limits for

Walter. Contemplating questions conjured up the grinding old feelings of confusion, greed and anger. Like seeing Mathias crazed and being forced to stand up to a man that seemed to be inhabited by something else, a spirit, a ghost? He shook his head while taking a deep breath.

In the end he couldn't help himself, "Getting in any caves down there?"

Bev was waiting for this, "Mathias has taken me around to a few and he showed me your map."

At the mention of "your map" Walter cringed.

"He's got the treasure bug," she said. "He thinks I can see more on the map than he can. He thinks I don't see him watch my every move out of the corner of his eye," Bev paused. "Well truth be told, he can't see the map move and light up the same as me. But he's getting on my nerves and he's coming across kind of obsessed."

Walter sat back and sidelined his snooping to make room for his fatherly advice role, "This thing is an adventure, but be careful. There is something going on that may not be too ordinary," he said, thinking he should be more emphatic. But he just let it lie.

"Walter, did you ever meet my mom?" Bev said.

"Your mom and dad topped the treasure hunt news for a bit after they found that treasure, but I never met either one. I only heard about your grandpa, but never met him."

"My mom has a kind of 6th sense. She sees and feels things differently than other people. She called to warn me about Mathias."

"Warn you?"

"Well, she said there were some forces, she calls them energies, that are working here and it could get over my head."

"Over your head?"

"I asked her if she had my back and she said something that

got my attention. She said, 'this one might be too big for me.'" Bev said.

Walter slumped down in his chair stunned, politely said goodbye, and hung up the phone.

∽

A FEW MINUTES LATER, Bev picked up her phone.

"Honey get on a plane and go see your friend Walter Talon. My group sees that he has something about this map thing that you need. He doesn't know he has it, but we think it will surface. Go tomorrow," Alice said.

The call ended and Bev sat back, looked up and said, "Price, want to go to Virgin Gorda tomorrow?"

∽

THE SMALL CESSNA twin-engine jet sat on the tarmac at BNA, Nashville's International Airport. Price steered the Prius to the north end of the airport to an unmarked gate. He punched in the four-digit code, then drove around and parked in front of a small office with the simple sign, "Air Travel Partners." Bev eyed the eight-seater jet. She and Price had seats 7 and 8. They were the last to reserve and she'd be sitting in the jump seat in front of the bathroom door for the first leg of the flight.

Six passengers were headed non-stop to St. Barth in the leeward islands. All six were seated when Bev and Price boarded the plane. Four faced each other across a table set with white linen. The seats were beige leather with plush armrests. Three bench seats were occupied by two passengers, leaving one plus the jump seat, which Bev insisted on taking. They buckled-up and lifted off. The Cessna citation had short-field takeoff and landing capabilities and was just barely small enough to land in the challenging conditions at St. Barths. They settled in for the first leg.

"When did you tell Walter that we'd arrive?" Price said.

"Well, I didn't exactly tell him when," Bev replied.

"So, the plan is we meet him tomorrow?" he said.

"Not exactly," she said.

"What does 'not exactly' mean?"

"It means I haven't told him we are coming to see him, yet."

Price sat back in the plush leather seat and chuckled under his breath. The drone of the jet engines filled the air and the six other passengers all sat reading or flipping through magazines.

The PA system crackled, "Welcome to Air Travel Partners charter jet service. We're happy to have you joining us this morning. We're traveling in a Cessna Citation Latitude twin-engine turboprop at an airspeed of 400 miles an hour. The range of this jet is 2300 miles. We'll be landing in five hours on St Barth, refueling then off to Tortola in the British Virgin Islands. Please let us know if we can do anything to make your flight more comfortable."

Price slipped off his loafers and shifted slightly in his seat.

"So, what is the plan. I mean the plan for meeting up with Walter. And, what exactly are we going there to get?" Price said in a whisper to Bev.

"The plan is to call him when we land to figure out a time," Bev paused. "Second, I don't know why we're going. Mom said Walter has something we need. I've never seen her worry this much about anything. I'll call her from Tortola. She'll have more insight then."

Price looked stunned like this was Melissa from college all over again. Yeah, there are spirits and unknowns in the world, but he was quite sure his own spirit was all he needed.

CHAPTER
TWENTY-TWO

P rice walked out the front door of the small rental cottage at Leverick Bay, opened the car door and tossed a small bag onto the back seat. He got in the driver's side and looked over to see Bev slide in the front seat next to him. It had been a pleasant morning but the vibe was a little guarded.

"I know this appears to be a wild goose-chase, but you're going to love looking around this island," Bev said. The walk down to the Caves isn't flashy, but the view of the island chain from up there is spectacular and it changes all the way down to the water."

Bev loved the islands and was glad to be back again even for another short visit. She was still un-packing the baggage of college life, and Wall Street, and these islands had a way of relaxing her. She knew this was a hard sell-job on Price, and it may not be her finest hour of relationship building, but wired in her brain was the idea from childhood, *if you get a chance to drop everything and take off to the islands, do it.* She forgot that Price wasn't wired for that. His wiring was more like, *if you get a chance to get on stage and sing the new song you just wrote, do it.*

He put a couple of client projects on hold at the last minute for this trip. She was sure it wasn't for love of the islands. He was smitten and not only could she tell that, but she was feeling the same way.

"Tonight we're going to CocoMaya right on the beach," Bev said. "It's a kind of Caribbean food with a touch of Asian. It's unique, and I can promise you mister singer-songwriter they don't have one of these in Nashville."

"Do they have a stage and guitar?" Price said. "I may need to loosen them up with a little Dixie Stomp!"

"We can make that happen," she said and they both laughed.

"Now, what's the full story on Walter? I still remember something about, 'that's why we came.'"

"I jumped the gun and assumed he was here on Gorda, but he was home in Alabama," she paused. "But Mom said to go right down to that island and see Walter tomorrow. So that's what we did. It was a knee-jerk reaction, I admit."

"Let's talk about this 'Mama thing' you've got going," Price said. "What else do you do just like your mom?"

"Look, I know she's the mama-duck and I grew up following behind her. I'm working on cutting the cord," she said.

"Okay that's admirable, but is this a thing where if mama drinks green tea at three every day, you drink green tea at three? If mama buys a pineapple once a week, you do too? If mama leaves all the lights on at night...well fess up, little girl," Price said.

"Guilty as charged, judge," Bev laughed and reached over and snuggled her cheek in the small of his neck. "But I'm kinda stuck on you," she whispered. "And Mama's not."

They drove on the windy road snagging intermittent glimpses of the Caribbean Sea for a few minutes, then Price said, "I've always thought it's best to be yourself, because the somebody you might want to be might be already taken."

They drove through the small settlement heading south along the coast with some light chatter, but mostly taking in the view.

On a straight stretch of road Price said, "Okay what's the Walter story and the plan to meet with him."

"He's flying commercial from Fort Lauderdale late tomorrow, so we'll knock around and go see him the day after," she said.

"What did he say when you told him we flew down here to see him?"

"I didn't tell him that. I said we were down here for a quick get-away, and thought we'd drop by."

"Does Mama tell white lies like that one?" he said.

"I think there's a fine line between downright lying and small...very small fibs," she said.

"Really. That leaves me only one option," he said. "I'm putting you on 'truth-probation' Miss Bev Dahl."

They pulled into the parking lot high above the rock formation on the beach known as the Caves. Bev leaned over and gave Price another snuggle.

"I submit, judge, to your every command," she said with a giggle.

THE NEXT MORNING they walked onto the pier at Leverick Bay and stood by the fuel bay until the forty-foot wave-runner pulled up. Before stepping in, Price looked at the two outboard Honda engines at 300 horsepower each, and compared them to the 115 on his lake boat. Contrary to being impressed, he wondered what was out there around these islands that needed that much fire-power.

Their first stop was the small marina on Cooper Island, then to an isolated beach on the south side of Peter Island, and next lunch at Myett's Grill in Cane Garden Bay. The bulk of the British Virgin Islands circle an area called the Sir Francis Drake Channel, forming a barrier of protection from high winds and rough seas.

"My Grandpa used to say, 'each morning you leave the most beautiful place you've ever been and each afternoon you sail into the most beautiful place you've ever been.' I guess I have to agree," Bev said.

"Yep, I could get used to this," Price answered.

Two days later they sat in the rental car in the driveway of Walter's house for a minute and neither one made a move to open the door.

"Guess I'm ready," Bev said.

"Are you expecting a big deal in there?" Price said.

"This map thing may be a little bigger than you know about, up to this point," she said.

"Is Walter an 'okay' guy?" he asked.

"Yeah he is, but the last time I was here the map thing sent him off the deep-end. He might have been a little crazed by his time owning it," she said.

"Like Mathias is getting?"

"I think Walter was glad to get rid of it," she said.

"Maybe we should leave it in the car. Not take it in."

"Let's leave it in the tube. If we can tell that things are deteriorating, we won't bring it out," she said.

Walter stood inside the screen door as they approached. He wore a courteous smile leading the way to the living room. The view was just as Bev remembered it, a panoramic view of the bay at North Sound. Richard Branson's Necker Island lay just outside the bay with open ocean beyond. Price held on to the tube while trying to make it inconspicuous, but he caught Walter looking at it, and saw his smile fade and his demeanor change.

"Thanks for making time for us. I'm introducing Price to the Islands for a few days," Bev said.

They chit-chatted about island life and what Nashville was like this time of year. Finally Bev mustered the confidence to get to the meat of the visit.

"I've been exploring a lot of caves in Tennessee, lately. The complexity of the channels running above and below and on all sides is mind-bending," she said.

Walter shrugged but made no comment.

"Mathias thinks I can help him find this treasure, but it's all getting a little weird," she continued.

Walter diverted his attention from Bev and looked out the picture window.

"Yes, I know the whole thing can get weird. I'd offer to help you but I gave up fooling with that map," he said. "Sometimes I think I should have burned it and not even given it to Mathias."

Price reached for the tube. He was breaking protocol by jumping into the conversation. He knew he'd been brought down there to be only a spectator.

"Well, you've got a second chance, Mr. Talon."

He flipped the stopper-lid off the tube and cajoled the map out.

"Here's the famous map that's driving my step-father crazy, not to mention my girlfriend, and everybody else it seems," Price said.

There was no shock on Walter's face the way Bev had anticipated. Instead he sat back and watched Price unroll it on the dining table. Walter took the few steps to the table and looked intently at the details of the map.

"It's completely changed since I first saw it. The locations that I explored are gone and the north/south orientation has nearly switched completely," Walter said. "I don't know if this whole thing comes from heaven or deep-down in the underworld."

"Walter, when I go in the caves, I get clear feelings which way to go," Bev said. "If I try offshoots that are wrong, the feeling just goes flat."

"I have to be honest, I don't know what all this is, but Bev, you can see more of this than anybody else," Walter said. "I thought it was merely an intriguing artifact when I gave it to Mathias, but it may be dangerous. You need to be careful," he paused. "Hey Price, you want to burn this friggin' map right now?"

"Light it up!"

Just then a soft rumble started in the floor. Walter looked around noticing a shift in the air around him along with a musty smell filling the room. Then he felt the rumble dissipate just as quickly as it arrived. But for Bev the room seemed to explode. She felt the roar transition into a loud screech and then she could almost hear a train crashing through the walls. She got dizzy, staggered toward a chair and into a side table. The lamp on the table started to tip over and to her own amazement, she had the presence to reach for it before it hit the ground. Off balance and ready to tumble to the floor, she bent her knees in a crouching position to gain stability. That's when she noticed a small object on the floor that was knocked off the table. She stooped over and picked it up. It fit comfortably in the palm of her hand, and as her fingers closed around it, the rumbling stopped abruptly.

She held it under the lamp to examine it. A simple wooden cross with what appeared to be a carving of a royal coat of arms, but she wasn't sure.

Price saw Bev stagger, went into high alert, and was poised and ready for whatever came next. But nothing came next. It was quiet.

No one spoke a single word as Price rolled and put the map back in the tube. Then he spoke like a friendly, father figure to Bev.

"The biggest favor you ever did for Mathias was take this map. Now do yourself that same favor. Bury it, or throw it over the side of the boat, or throw it out of an airplane. But, get rid of it. The energy on that thing is coming from a bad, angry place," he paused. "No good will come of it."

Looking down, Price inched his way toward the front door. He saw Walter start to lose his composure and knew it was time to head for the trenches.

"It'll turn you and everything you have into a mess, and just think what...." Bev cut Walter off.

"Thank you Walter. Your thoughts are extremely helpful, and we will think carefully about your advice," Bev said as she followed Price through the front door. She tilted her head back and said over her should, "Come see us in Nashville sometime."

Price opened the car door for Bev, jumped in the driver's side and drove down the driveway without a word. At the stop sign onto the main road, Price stopped the car.

"Come see us in Nashville? I thought you lived in California or New York, or wherever?" he said.

She looked over with a sheepish grin, "I might live in Nashville someday. Who knows?"

"Who says we'd let you in?" he joked.

~

BACK IN CALIFORNIA, Alice spoke first to start the phone meeting of the small, select group from the Paranormal Institute.

"Bev found an object in the islands as we thought she would. I've looked at its energy and what I can see is a lot of spiritual vibe around it. Even though it seems small it has great power," Alice said while the group listened tuning into her thoughts.

"I see spiritual too, some sort of cross, I think. It's not ancient, maybe three or four hundred years old," Elizabeth chimed in. "Around 1650 or so. This may sound funny, but I see a gold glow at its center and simmering around the periphery is suffering and pain, but the pain stays weak next to the bright glow."

Then a new voice joined the conversation, "Hi Alice I'm Danya. You may not remember me but you took a class from me a few years back," she said. "I'm the director of the Institute, so thought I'd sit in on the session today."

"I do remember your class," Alice said.

"I see there is some challenging energy that your daughter is facing. There is the power of many beings at work here, which can overtake a single soul," Danya said. "I've taken the liberty to communicate with Bev on the astral plane. Her energy is positive and she is staying grounded. She knows that if she loses grounding, she will likely be vulnerable. What are you seeing Keri?"

"The object Bev found, and by the way I see it as a cross too, is important and as long as she has it in her possession, she is insulated from the dark energy," Keri said.

"The bad energy wants it back, though," Elizabeth chimed in. "It looks like it was a companion for the map for a long time, but got separated until now."

Okay. Hold on to the cross...hold on to the cross...hold on to the cross, Alice thought over and over, trying to direct her thoughts toward Bev.

CHAPTER
TWENTY-THREE

"Do you want to burn this relic from some old, long-dead dreamers, or keep the melodrama going?" Price asked.

"Do we have to talk about the dumb-old map?" Bev replied.

"Well since we haven't even mentioned it since we left Walter, it might be time to decide to love it or leave it," Price said.

"Can we just leave it in the tube for now?" Bev said.

Bev acted like she didn't care and couldn't be bothered by this whole thing, but that was a lie. Every waking moment she was pondering the question of "love it or leave it." Even that understated her obsession. She dreamed about it from every perspective, failing and never solving the treasure hunt, succeeding and what to do with all those coins, again. What if it got worse and she were hurt or Price, Branson, Mathias were injured.

There was a mentor in her dream last night, and the memory of it haunted her. She clearly knew what was said, but as she tried to grasp the words in the dream, each time they slipped away under a veil of clouds. She could not put it together in any logical sequence, still, she knew the kernel of it all, not the thoughts but the essence of what this dream-guide brought to her. She knew, *hold on to the cross.*

The jet engines purred along, piercing through a thirty-thousand-foot blue sky for the next hour, on the trip to Nashville. Bev thought about Price, thought about the friendship between the two of them. She dated in college but nothing serious. Did she even know how to move to the next step with a man? She looked out the window at a blanket of white clouds. *Not really.*

A couple of sorority sisters had it down and were engaged and ready to tie the knot at graduation. She felt that old attitude of, *how boring is that?* She chuckled to herself. *Maybe it's Mom and Dad's fault. After all, they didn't show much role modeling with getting divorced and all. And then there is Silicon Valley. I mean after all, it's a one-of-a-kind place. Who could be normal there, digital everything. Oh great, then next, right in the middle of Wall Street, and money grubbing bankers. How could a girl be normal?*

Price nodded off to sleep and the plane continued to skid through the ozone layer back to Nashville's Music City. A blubbery cumulous cloud engulfed the plane and thick fog chased the light from the sky. *Okay, the pity-party is over, Little Miss Victim of societal abuse and neglect. You studied economics and those girls studied getting-hitched. Step-up and make this happen*, she thought. *I don't know what fish Grandpa, but I'm going to fry some here-and-now with Price.*

She could see no reason to keep chasing this whole map thing. Maybe burning it was the right thing and just try to learn how to be with the guy she can't keep her eyes off of. Give it back to Mathias? *Why not?* She thought.

Later Price woke, looked over and said, "I think Walter has got some exaggerated ideas of this cave thing. Those caves aren't that scary. If you don't grow up around the dark and cold underground, I guess it would be creepy. Mathias didn't spend any time there until now. He and Walter are just intimidated and making up this 'bad angry place' stuff. Let's go rattle this tree and see what shakes out."

Bev nodded and mouthed the words, *okay but*, under her breath. She felt a guilty pang knowing there was more to this... and a lot more than Price was bargaining for. But his attitude switch from "throw it out the window" to "see what shakes out" worried her.

She wanted to dial up her mother. No, she wanted to sit in front of the fire and drink a cup of mint tea with her mother and be safe with everything easy.

BEV WOKE to see a mid-morning sun peek through the half-drawn curtains. She rubbed her eyes with both hands while making her way into the kitchen. Price stood at the breakfast table with the map spread out and a puzzled look on his face.

Bending over slightly, he gave her a peck on the lips and said, "Can you make anything of this?"

As she touched a point on the map, she could see an image forming around a tiny pulse of light. As the image became clearer, she noticed Price still squinting. She knew he was not seeing that same image clarity.

"Looks like a word. I don't know." She leaned closer. "I think it says something like 'Gizzard.' Is that a word?"

"Yep, it's part of a bird's stomach. Is that all it says?"

"That's all I see," she said. "Does it mean anything to you?"

"Has the map shown words before? I thought it was just lines and directions."

"That's mostly what I've seen. Honestly, Mathias never gave

me full access to it, so I don't know," she said. "Price, are you seeing that word?"

He looked up and paused, "No. Just a fuzzy image," he said. "Is there anything else, another word or lines, or anything?"

"Not right now. Maybe after I have a cup of coffee it'll play Beethoven's fifth symphony," she quipped.

"Yeah, I'll pour one and we'll see."

Bev took her coffee and made a bee-line to the front porch and the wicker rocking chair. She was determined that the day would unfold without the map as the focal point. She rested her cup on the side table and put her feet up on the ottoman, when her phone rang. Caller ID flashed "Conquistador." Letting it ring two more times, she contemplated whether or not to answer Branson's call. *No, clearly no*, she thought. On the fourth ring she punched the "talk" button and answered.

"Hi Sis," he said. "Those morons down in San Jose are holding out on my permit for the museum. I've got thousands of dollars of furniture and pedestals coming and I can't even think about opening the doors till I get that permit," he said.

"Good morning, Branson. And other than your immense, first-world cataclysmic disaster, how is life treating you?" she said.

"I guess, all right. Did you talk to Mom yesterday?"

"Yep, I called her when we touched down in Nashville."

"Good. Cause she's in alarm-mode over this treasure hunt you're on. Her group of psycho-whackos got her in a frenzy," he said. "I have to admit, this woo-woo stuff is a little much."

So he wanders around San Francisco dressed up like a fifteenth-century caballero, and this woo-woo stuff is too much? I can't stand this. Please god, take me. Take me now, she thought.

Price appeared at the doorway to the porch, "Is that Branson?" he asked. Bev nodded. "Tell him to get on a plane. I may need some help with this treasure hunt."

Bev rolled her eyes, "Price wants you to come out and help him...and me I guess."

"Tell him to bring Buzzy," Price added.

Dead-pan into the phone Bev said, "Bring Buzzy."

Two days later on Sunday, Price pulled around to the private airport gate and Branson and Buzzy jumped into the Prius. Two large suitcases barely squished into the trunk.

Price said, "You brought a ton of stuff?"

"We're doing battle. I'll need the right outfits," Branson replied.

They got Buzzy settled in the back seat.

"So, are we treasure hunting, cave dwelling, or just what am I doing here?" Branson said.

"Everybody having anything to do with this map is going whacky," Price replied. "I know more about these caves than any of them. The way I look at it, you and I can make short work of this and see what's at the end of this rainbow," He paused. "Oh yeah, and Buzzy too."

"I'm in," Branson said. "Where do things stand right now?"

"We still have the map and I'm spending some time getting familiar with it. Bev sees a word forming on the map that says, Gizzard. She doesn't know what that means, so I'm looking closer to see if anything else triggers a clue," Price said.

Just then the word "Gizzard" reverberated in his thoughts. *Gizzard, Gizzard, what is it about that word*, he thought.

"What about Gizzard's Peak?" he blurted out.

Branson turned to look at Price, "What?"

"Gizzard's Peak. It's an outcropping we used to climb on when I was in high school. No wait a minute, before high school. That kid I hung out with...his dad used to drive us up there, bring some sandwiches, in the Spring when the water was running. That's the time there is a water fall at Gizzard's Peak. We'd get muddy as all-get-out," Price paused to take a breath. "I'll bet that map is telling us to look at Gizzard's Peak."

~

Price took both suitcases from the trunk and rolled them into the spare room while Branson directed Buzzy to the grass in the front yard. Bev shrugged, but put on a happy face to greet Branson.

"I've got a cool glass of Sauvignon Blanc on the screen porch waiting for you," Bev said.

"It's only two in the afternoon in California," Branson said. "But I guess I can rise to the occasion."

They sat and took a sip when Price poked his head through the kitchen door.

"Branson, come in here and look at the map. See if you can make sense of anything."

The three of them stood over the kitchen table. Price looked at Bev and said, "Still no other words, just Gizzard?" She shook her head. "How about you, Branson. See anything?"

"I see a spot there but I don't see any words," Branson said, and gave a nonchalant glance toward Bev as if she were in possession of a secret... in charge of the mystery.

"I'll bet a dime to a dollar that our next stop is Gizzard's Peak," Price bellowed.

~

Price hurried everybody through breakfast and even walked Buzzy around the yard. He made sure they each had a second pair of shoes and a light jacket. After loading Buzzy in the back seat of the pickup truck with Bev, they took off.

"So I guess you know where we're going. How did you find it? On Google?" Bev said.

"No. This is guerrilla warfare. It's over Google's head. I called that kid Jimmy's dad and asked him. He acted like he was excited I even remembered the place and was interested in finding it. Anyway, it's back in the woods and a little tricky getting there. It's fifteen miles but they'll be slow-miles, maybe some farm gates and a creek-crossing or two," Price said. "I mentioned caves and his dad told me there are cave networks all over, and some of the simple sinkholes can lead to tunnels. Some are dead-ends and others can go for a while."

"How do these old guys know about all the caves," Branson said.

"Back then there weren't any shopping centers, or internet, and not everybody had TV, especially back in the country," Price said. "And it wasn't cool to drink beer all day like it is today, so they found stuff to do."

THE FIFTEEN MILES TOOK AN HOUR. When they stepped out of the car there was nothing to see but trees and scrubby underbrush.

"Think if we go this way, we'll run into the cliffs," Price said as he pointed into the woods.

"Cliffs? I thought it was a peak," Branson said.

"It's the highest point around here, but really it's just some cliffs sticking up," Price said.

"Is there a path to follow?" Bev asked.

"From the air, the path is probably visible. In fact, we would probably see a bunch of these sink holes and cave entrances flying over, but for now let's follow Buzzy, over there...that way," Price said.

Buzzy was well ahead with his nose to the ground and tail wagging. Price talked Branson into leaving the metal helmet in the truck, but he was still slowed down by the metal shin guards strapped to his spindly legs...always prepared in case the Indian warrior, Tecumseh, appeared from behind a tree. Bev's agile stride kept her in the lead just behind Buzzy. When she caught up to him, he was lapping up a drink from a quiet trickle of water lazily meandering through the woods. By the time Price uttered, "let's follow that stream to the source," Buzzy was bounding from rock to rock.

They caught up with Buzzy, and he was circling a small spot at the top of the cliffs. When Branson looked up, Buzzy opened his mouth and uttered a muted 'victory bark.'

"Good boy, Buzzy," Branson yelled.

"Everybody take a direction and spread out," Price said. "Look for a group of rocks that might be hiding a cave entrance or even a sinkhole.

Nobody had paid much attention back at the house, when Bev slipped the map into the truck. They paid less attention when she stuck it under her arm for the hike. Mathias treated the map like the holy grail, referring to it constantly. These guys ignored it, which made Bev nervous. She resented the map because of the power and energy it held...a force she couldn't understand. But above all, she respected it, and its power. She meandered through the woods for a hundred yards or more and then out of curiosity, she stopped and unrolled the map on a flat grassy spot.

With small rocks holding the corners down, she scanned the whole map, then drew her attention to the spot with the word "Gizzard" laying on the page. She stared at it waiting for the letters to pulsate and standout from the lines. She kept waiting...and waiting. The map just laid there. Nothing changed. Finally, she rolled it back up and began wandering around looking for clues to a possible cave entrance.

While watching Buzzy sniff for clues, she heard, "Hey everybody. Bev, Branson get over here. I found an entrance."

Bev reached in the pocket of her jacket and let her fingers wrap around the small wooden cross, glad she remembered to bring it. Then she followed the sound of Price's voice and arrived just ahead of Branson.

"Help me pull these bushes out of the way," Price said. "Look in back of that rock. It's clearly a cave entrance."

They clawed their way down a rock-strewn path, and to a vertical entrance to a cold, dark passageway. Firing up the flashlights, they struggled to squeeze past the sandstone cap layer and finally made it to a limestone tunnel. Bev heard the metal scrapping sound from Branson's leg armor, but shrugged it off. Buzzy was in the lead, but stayed just in front of the light beam.

"This has got to be where the map was taking us. Am I right or what?" Price said. "I've got two big lamps that run on batteries. Let's regroup and bring them back tomorrow. They'll light up this whole place."

Bev put both hands around the tube and felt for vibrations or movement, or an energy, anything that might correspond with Price and his idea that this is the place. Nothing was coming from the map.

MATHIAS TOOK two hours to find his way back home. He had followed Price's truck when they left the house and made it past two turn-offs, but lost them after that. He banged the stirring wheel of his truck in frustration. *How could I be so stupid*, he thought. His strategy was to stay back so Price wouldn't recognize his truck and know he was following them.

The hourlong trek back through the country gave Mathias time to re-tool his strategy. When he finally made it to the blacktop and Highway 41, he drove straight to a small car lot south of Nashville. He had never bought a car there, but he figured they may have just what he needed. After a short thirty-minute look around, he got in his truck and turned it north on 41 with the salesman close behind in his new 1991 Ford F-150. It was a two-tone model with a white hood and brown door panels. He got a good price because it looked well-worn, and his own brief inspection concurred.

The salesman pulled in the driveway next to Mathias, handed him the keys, climbed into the service vehicle that had followed them from the car lot, and was gone in minutes. Mathias stood and looked at the two trucks side-by-side. The contrast was laughable. But Matthias was not laughing much these days. *They'll never recognize me in this piece of junk*, he thought. *But what if things get dicey and I get too close. They could recognize me through the windows,* he thought.

Walking in the house and into the small basement he used for storage, he started rummaging through the dusty plastic bins. Opening one after another, he kept going until he suddenly stopped, pulled an old hat out and slapped it on his head. Walking over to the small mirror in the half-bath, he gazed at a sloppy old man reflecting back at him. He pulled the hat down lower over his forehead. *Yep they'll never recognize me in this*, he thought.

Mathias was up, dressed and ready to go at six the next morning. He drove by Price's house to see the farm truck still sitting empty in the driveway. Then he and the old F-150 rattled back to the main road. When the group began to load into their truck, he took a chance they would go the same route to the new cave. He drove to the first big turn, off the blacktop, and waited. The traffic was light so when the group appeared in his review mirror, Mathias pulled his hat down and slumped in his seat.

The next morning the farm truck turned, and at the top of the first hill, stopped to open the make-shift wire gate. Mathias slowly shifted gears to drive position and turned onto the dirt road far enough behind them to not be seen.

The ground was still damp from the evening dew, so the dust was minimal as Price blasted down the dirt road. Bev looked over at him and thought about her mom and the warnings of caution.

She texted her mom last night and filled her in on the new adventure. Alice replied back with, *Price is a man on a mission. Let him play this out. Keep an eye on that map, though. There's some bad energy around.* She told her mother that Mathias is staying away and maybe he's forgotten about this whole thing. She replied, *he is very close and has not forgotten anything. He's a big worry, and wants the map back. My group is watching him.*

The farm truck barreled through open fields then entered a stand of trees where Price stopped the truck at a small stream-crossing to give Buzzy a short walk. Mathias was in close pursuit, and just before he entered the tree line, he saw them. Without braking he veered left into the field, drove about two hundred yards, stopped and pulled out a shovel from the truck bed. He was a farmer just doing a little work on the field. Who would think otherwise? Buzzy looked up and out through the woods, Price and the group didn't notice a thing. They were focused and on a mission.

Price made his own road through the woods to Gizzard's Peak. They unloaded the lights and carried them over to the entrance of the cave.

Bev made a nod toward Branson and said, "I don't think

that's going to work in the cave." She referred to the wide-brim three-corner hat with large feather, he was wearing over the metal breast-plate and black tights.

"You mean the feather?" Branson asked.

"Well, yes the feather," pausing. "I think the breast-plate will come in handy," she said with a muffled smirk.

Price turned away to hide his ear-to-ear grin and struggled not to laugh out loud.

THEY TRUDGED through the narrow entrance to the cave with the lighting canisters in tow. Branson trailed in last. When he arrived, he placed the big light on a rock, flipped the switch and illuminated a large cavern, while Buzzy barked at the sight of it all. Bev scanned the room and focused on a group of stalagmites a few feet away. As Branson stepped in front of the light, Bev got a glimpse of the mud covering the entire right side of him.

"Branson!" Bev shouted.

"I guess these leather-sole boots don't have much traction on slippery rocks," he said.

"The king and queen will banish you from the fiefdom," she giggled while Price pretended not to hear.

"That'll be enough of that," Branson snapped.

Price went straight to the illuminated wall and began to examine the mineral drippings from a million years of slow, steady trickle. The flutes hung from the ceiling and along the walls like organ pipes randomly organized into a celestial pageant of gray and brown with shadowed crevices bleeding into black. He took a deep breath and imagined the pipes bellowing out a Bach masterpiece melody, gently massaged by haunting harmony. He took another deep breath as he reached out to touch the minuscule undulations of the smooth surface.

He saw these formations first as a kid of nine or ten, but still marveled at the intricate detail of the craftsman's work.

His eyes dropped toward the ground, overlooking a couple of beginner stalagmites. He scanned the ground looking for clues he could use. Branson trained the second flood light on the opposite wall and discovered a tunnel hidden in the shadows. He ducked into it. His flashlight lit the path ahead for Buzzy and the two explorers cautiously moved forward.

About ten minutes passed when Branson re-emerged into the bright cavern. Bev and Price looked up with a questioning stare on both their faces.

"Dead-end," Branson announced.

"Did you look up high and on the sides for hidden tunnels?" Price asked.

Branson took a few steps over to a sitting-size rock and plopped down. He took a deep breath and let himself notice the refreshing "taste" of the air in the cavern. That tunnel got dryer and mustier the deeper he pressed into its depth.

Noticing that deep breath, Bev said, "It's wetter in this part of the cave, so the air is better...cleaner, and feels lighter."

"Looks like your hat made it through that tunnel and back out," Bev said.

"I took the hat off outside the tunnel before I went in," he said. "You know, the feather and all."

Bev looked at the mud caked on Branson and saw no sign of it drying out. For the rest of the morning they looked high and low for tunnels or passages that offered direction or clues, but found nothing. Just before noon they flipped the flood lights out and headed to the entrance.

Mathias watched from a small hill a few hundred yards from the cave during the morning, but as the hours passed and with no sign of the group, he became bolder and slithered his way to the entrance. The intrigue as well as his curiosity overwhelmed him and drove him to peek into the cave entrance. He didn't see any light emerging, but did hear the echo of voices in time for him to retreat back to his hilltop perch. He watched them snack on the packed lunch and could hear some of the banter...but not all of it.

"This is No-where's-ville," Branson said.

"Are you getting any vibe from the map or any other cosmic channels, Bev?" Price asked.

Bev took another bite. She compared the feelings and information that flooded into her brain when the map was "speaking" to her. And she knew the flat feeling of nothing, whenever she took the wrong path and the map went silent. Not eager to explain this whole thing, she knew her words would fall flat on this audience. Besides, although she knew what she felt and somehow understood it with clarity, she didn't really know what it was or how to describe it.

Finally she answered, "Not a thing."

Bev's words echoed through the forest, and Mathias heard it loud and clear. He sat back and smiled.

Over the next week, Price and Branson drove back to Gizzard's Peak every day with the same routine just to probe and explore, to see if anything sparked an idea or direction to follow. The summer heat was beginning to blanket the Cumberland basin and although the old farm truck had a new radiator, carburetor, and brakes, it had no air conditioner. Windows down and inching along the dirt roads was a lesson in southern living that

Price knew well, but it felt like Marine Corps boot-camp to Branson, a bit of new-recruit training that he did not embrace gracefully.

The seventy-five degrees in the cave was a welcome relief each day that they both looked forward to. After a few trips, Branson routinely tossed his protective armor in the bed of the truck for the ride out, but he would only enter the cave with full gear draped over him, poised and ready like a Marvel superhero.

The clanging metal skirt protecting his mid-section from an enemy's cutting sidewinding sword, clanged and echoed through the cave.

Hard to bend down, heavy to carry through the uneven passages of the cave, the armor clung to Branson like cellophane on a ham sandwich. It was like a kid blinded by the sun directly in his eyes, but with his hat on backwards, faithful to his self-image, an image that nobody else cared about.

On the third day, Price looked over at Branson and said, "I'm pretty sure that the chance of an unsheathed steal-blade belonging to a perilous enemy coming your way is right around zero."

Branson didn't break stride, didn't look over, and acted like he didn't hear it. In spite of everything the search continued.

BEV TALKED to her mother daily and the advice from Alice was to give the boys free-rein to wear themselves out. Like Bev, Alice had no current premonitions about the treasure hunt. The energy field they were monitoring, felt flat. She continued to apprise Bev that Mathias was not fading away. She could see his interest as strong. She did not, however, mention to Bev that he was following the farm truck every day to watch every move from his hidden perch, a fact that seemed to be off her radar.

One day after a hearty lunch of canned beef stew, sitting at the cave entrance in the bright southern sun, Branson proclaimed, "Okay, how about we go to Memphis and visit Elvis."

"Yeah man, chasing this treasure is getting old. We're getting nowhere," Price said.

Bev sat back and tried to look uninterested as the boys expressed their frustration. She could feel the "give-up, we're beat," vibe dripping from the pores of these worn-out cavers.

Mom is so smart. They are wearing themselves out, she thought. Her main thought was just how best to give the map back to Mathias. She stood up and poured another round of Ridge Pinot Noir only to see the glasses drained quickly by these beaten-down adventurers.

CHAPTER
TWENTY-FOUR

The guest room door was shut in the morning, so nobody noticed that Branson left early. Bev was up around six and managed to drain a half pot of coffee while sitting on the screen-porch. Although she woke thinking about the map and the quest it had taken them on so far, her thoughts were straying. As she poured her third cup of coffee, the small matter of, "what was she going to do for the rest of her life," crept into her mind.

Earlier Price bolted up and out the door to the barn for some reason, so it was quiet with only a sleeping Buzzy, and a slight breeze to accompany Bev's daydreaming. She glanced over to the door to Branson's bedroom, and as usual, began the mental preparation for dealing with her little brother and his grand world of fantasy whenever he decided to presented himself.

Without warning, Buzzy lifted his head and gave a slightly muted bark. Bev thought nothing of it, but noticed he was up and moving to the outside screen for a better look into the yard. Another bark, and then Bev began to hear a low rumbling sound. The sound grew louder and Buzzy began a litany of barking punctuated by a few howls. Bev opened the screen door and walked out into a mysterious whirling wind and a deafening roar. She felt light-headed as fear seeped into her mind, with the first thought that this terrible map was striking them with a revenge for which she was sure she had no defense. She raised her arm to shield her face from a potential onslaught of retaliation. But no ephemeral, or spiritual foe materialized. Instead a giant roundish object was hovering over the flat area in the side yard, about a hundred feet away.

A helicopter? What are the police doing here? she thought. Price stood next to the barn shielding his face from the dust whipped up by this giant bird as its wheels settled on the grass. When the door opened, a pilot emerged, jerked his headset off with his left hand, while simultaneously with his right hand, slapping a black three-cornered hat, with a distinctive feather, onto his head.

Bev squared off, planted both feet in the grass and waving her arms, yelled at the top of her lungs, "Branson, you can't do this! Stop! I'm telling you to stop this insane junk."

The blade on top of the helicopter kept turning and the engine drowned out all communication, with exception of the arm waving. Branson moved away from the rotors, raised his arms and enthusiastically waved back to Bev, assured of her fascination, delight, and intrigue in his morning surprise.

Price started to walk slowly around the machine, while Branson made his way to greet Bev in the yard. Price could see Bev pointing her forefinger at Branson and waving it in his face. Even from a distance, he could see her in full lecture mode, her lips in fast motion, and words flying like bats swarming a tree.

Bev turned and marched into the house. Branson shook his head in bewilderment as Price approached.

"It's stripped down to make room for the equipment," Branson said, turning his attention to Price.

"Equipment? What equipment are you talking about?" Price said.

"GPS, sensors, and the thermal cameras," Branson said. "No room for the wine cooler and the deep freeze," he quipped.

"What's all this for, anyway? I'm not sure what you're talking about," Price said.

"Aerial mapping. We need to find those sinkholes and zero-in on cave entrances. I'm talking about places you'd never see even standing next to them, because the underbrush covers 'em up," Branson said.

"Okay, let's backup," Price said. Where did you get that helicopter? And who is flying it?"

"I'm flying it. Well, Clifton is co-pilot. He works for the charter company and comes along with the rental."

"Branson, talk to me here. How is it that you are flying that machine?" Price said.

"Well, my abilities never came up because that 'machine' as you call it, is a little too big to fly into most caves around here," Branson said. "I'm licensed for this Airbus H Series in all fifty states. Licensed and insured! The real deal. I've got it till sunset today, and it cost a healthy handful of pieces of eight to get it, so we need to get airborne ASAP.

BEV WAS SITTING in the kitchen when the guys walked in. She was simmering down and was letting herself realize that her reaction was mostly from getting scared...evil, dark energy, and then the police. *Okay I get that I was scared, but I don't need this scaring-me-to-death business to keep going on. I need to straighten Branson out...or maybe Mom can give him a talking to*, she thought.

Branson boldly walked up to Bev, "Sorry, big Sis, for the

scare. I can see how it turned out a bit freaky. I'll clear this kind of move with you in the future."

Bev nodded but stayed silent, not brooding but just from of lack of any coherent response.

"Branson's got some high-tech equipment that he's thinking will give us an aerial picture of sinkholes and cave entrances," Price said.

"There's an imaging spectrometer that will give us a color-coded map of the land surface," Branson said, "and from there we can see what cave entrances might be hidden from view."

"Is that going to help?" Bev asked.

"Well it won't hurt."

Bev sat in silence before bursting into a shriek, "Christ Branson, there is a list a mile long of things that won't hurt. I'm getting sick of this losing adventure. Maybe we should go visit Elvis. Anything but watching intrepid treasure hunters boldly go where no one else gives a flying-you-know-what about.

Branson and Price sat in silence looking at their feet and making no eye contact.

Branson breached the stillness, "We can print out a large format map, bring it back and see if any of the spots coordinate with the treasure map," he said. "If it does, at least we'll have another data point. If not, we can make lunch plans with Elvis."

BUZZY WAS LEFT GUARDING the map, while Bev and Price crawled into the back seats of the copter, pulled their seat belts tight, and hoped that Branson and Clifton could actually fly this eggbeater. The air smelled oily like a machine shop even with the forced air ventilation circulating. Bev felt the rotors surge as Branson push a lever forward on the front instrument panel and the wheels lifted off the turf.

Clifton's recent explanation of the process was clear and understandable, but left Bev still wondering if these high tech gadgets would be a game-changer or even help at all. The ground receded as they gained altitude, and the GPS instruments guided them to the area around Gizzard's Peak. An electronic grid was laid out and the camera started recording the ground below. It was all controlled by the computer leaving nothing for Price and Bev to do but take in the scenery below.

The Airbus had a flight time of only 3 hours and 35 minutes. Fifteen minutes from Nashville's Tune Airport to Price's farm, left a bit over three hours to fill in the grid. After two and a half hours, Clifton raised his left hand and pointed to the instrument panel directing Branson's gaze to the fuel gauge. Branson gave a slight nod, and straightened his headset microphone.

"Hey guys, we're going to fill in the last of this area map and then head back to the farm," he said. "We've got enough for a good taste of this whole deal. Call Elvis and reschedule, okay?"

By the time the chopper touched down, the wide format printer built into the cargo area had printed out a composite color-coded map as well as fourteen sector charts. Clifton neatly rolled them up and handed them to Price before Branson lifted the machine off the turf and the pilots headed back to the airport.

An hour later Branson walked in the kitchen, he grabbed the unopened grid maps and began to unroll them.

"I think the plan is to put the treasure map over these and see if any reaction happens," Branson proclaimed.

"I know what's going to happen for me. I'm going to want a beer," Price said.

"Yeah, right. Okay, Bev is going to do the heavy lifting to see if she gets a feeling, a noise, a smell, or a visual as we pinpoint the sinkhole locations," Branson quickly chimed in.

Bev's lips tightened into a smirk and her eyes rolled, with no effort to hide her skepticism and complete lack of enthusiasm. Map after map was positioned over and under for more than two hours.

One map slipped off the table and rolled onto the floor. Branson stooped down and coming up with it said to Bev, "Are you getting any feelings or sensations?"

"Actually, I am."

Branson perked up, "Terrific, what are you feeling?"

"I feel like if I don't get to the bathroom soon, I'm going to bust," she proclaimed.

Price instantly lifted his fist to his lips for a make-believe microphone and belted out the hit song *Hooked on a Feeling*. He sang "high on a believing," as he rolled into the 1970s B.J. Thomas hit that he frequently covered on stage. Bev danced her way down to the hall bathroom, while Branson sat in the corner alone and defeated.

The excitement of the helicopter and high tech had faded away by the time they finally gave up on the aerial maps. Bev thought about the futility of science in confluence with this energy thing going on, and how incompatible the two were. *Maybe this map stuff is science, just a science way above human understanding*, she thought, *or maybe not*. Her last thought before toppling off to sleep was how to get the map back to Mathias.

No LIGHT PEEKED through the closed windows at five in the morning as Bev stumbled to the bathroom. Her eyes began to focus in the low light, then rounding the corner she headed back to bed. She saw that the kitchen light was left on overnight. *Reach in there on the left and flip it off*, she thought. But appearing in the doorway, she was greeted by Prices' simple question,

"Are there any places that you can see lighting up on the map this morning?"

He was standing in front of the kitchen table with the treasure map unrolled, pointing to the cave entrance that she had explored with Mathias a month ago. He made no mention of the aerial maps, the grid, and the seeming dead-ends from yesterday.

To her surprise the markings around that map-point had changed. Additionally, the small glow of light at that spot had faded away. It was now just like all other places on the map.

She shook her head and answered Price, "It's all changed. The lines have moved and nothing is lighting up. This whole thing is screwy and I'm going back to bed."

AT EIGHT O'CLOCK Price's cell phone rang, "Hey Price, this is Jimmy. How have you been?"

"Uh, Jimmy?" Price drew out the name, hoping to have the identity of a Jimmy pop into his head.

"Jimmy Ingram. You called my dad asking about that old hike we used to make to that little bluff."

"Oh yeah. Good. Jimmy. All is good. It's been a long time. What you been up to?"

"I was teaching school, but now I'm selling insurance. I'm out in Hendersonville these days. Got a divorce. I guess things happen," he paused. "All good, though."

"Good, good to hear," Price said.

"I wanted to say hi, but also a little curious about you hiking around up there. You know there's nothing really up there but some scruffy farmland. You gonna build a subdivision or something?" he said.

"Nothing like that. Truth is I've been knocking around some caves lately," he paused, knowing that Jimmy knew full well that interest in crawling around limestone caves dropped off the radar before age sixteen, even for country boys. Cars, girls, beer. Caves weren't in the mix. Telling this guy about a map that lights up and changes all the time, and a pirate treasure waiting to be found, was not going to happen. So, he said the only thing that made sense, "I got a new California girlfriend that gets a kick out of caves."

"Okay, I get it. It's always about a girl," he said. "Nothing ever changes. I've got some time on my hands. Does she have a sister?"

Price knew he dodged the bullet and was ready to wrap up this friendly greeting-call with Jimmy Ingram.

"Take her over to Cumberland Caverns. They've got that all set up so you can see the big caverns but not get dirty. There's an upscale pizza place just outside the gate. A walk in the cave, a couple of pitchers. You'll be on your way to a productive date," Jimmy said. "California? Good work, buddy."

"Do you remember much about the caves? You know from the old days," Price asked.

"I know there are probably a thousand miles of caves around here. That is if anybody wanted to crawl around down there in the mud and cold. The rain melts the limestone. Add in a couple of million years and, voila, you got caves," Jimmy said.

"Yep, that sounds about right," Price said. "You have any favorites?" Price was probing just in the off-chance that some helpful info might plop in his lap.

"My favorites were always the dry ones, and then later the ones you could drive close to, so the beer cooler was close by,"

Jimmy said. "Linda liked the one that was closer to the highway. She didn't like how dark it got way out in the woods. Can't remember the name of that place. You remember Linda McComb, don't you? She's the one I ended up marrying, well divorced now."

"Yeah, she was a cool girl. Sorry to hear about that," Price said.

"Well, nice talking and doing some catchup," Jimmy said.

"Yeah, buddy, stay in touch." Price started to pull the phone from his ear and end the call when he heard Jimmy's voice.

"Gizzard's Crawl. That's the cave Linda liked. See you, man," Jimmy said and hung up.

Price stared at his phone for half a minute. The words, "Gizzard's Crawl," hung in the air in front of him. He was stunned.

CHAPTER
TWENTY-FIVE

Bev poured a cup of coffee and disappeared out the back door. This morning there was a light dew on the grass and the air had a touch of sparkle in it. She was walking the old cow path that wound around next to the fence line till it circled back to the pasture. When arriving at the far gate, she stood and looked back at the house and the few brown and white Hereford head of cattle that dotted the field. The touch of coffee that sloshed around in the bottom of the cup was cold. She flung the cold java onto the grass, rested the cup on a fence post, and opened the back gate. She'd only walked to the back of the farm once with Price. *Just walk till you get tired then turn around and come back*, she thought. Feeling no rush, she knew she was extending her twenty-minute stroll.

Once through the gate, Bev started to feel a release in her shoulders...her temples let go the tightness, and to her surprise the distant woods brightened and came into a sharper focus. The cow trail narrowed and mostly surrendered to the field grass encroaching before the trail disappeared altogether. Losing sight of the house, the fence line became her compass as she walked into an unknown world. *Unknown world...give me a break,* she whispered to herself. She stopped and laid her hand on the wire fence. Then reaching in her jacket pocket, she let her fingers wrap around the cold, flat silver disk. The slightly raised contours of this silver piece of eight were as familiar to her as any object she owned.

Bev inhaled the crisp morning air and with a hardy exhale, the image of Grandpa Richard shimmered in front of her eyes, not ghostly but more like a mirage. She did not feel concerned or even compelled to act or speak. Another mouthful of country air reinforced her resolve to be silent, be part of this place and time.

When Grandpa Richard finally spoke, she felt comforted with a simple, modest feeling of "knowingness." She felt like she "knew" her grandfather, not what he looked like or what he would say or what people said about him. She couldn't immediately describe it. When he spoke, it wasn't in words or sounds or even images. She just knew it.

"A fine kettle of fish," Grandpa said.

Expecting a profound utterance from this famed spirit, traveler, and treasure hunter, she laughed-out-loud. *Where was the deep meaning that comes from spirits who travel in time through the astral plane to be here and now...fine-tuning the mortal lives of the flailing souls they left behind.*

Bev pulled the coin from her pocket and held it out in front of her in the clear, country air.

"It's the coin you gave me when I was four. I still have it," she said.

In Bev's reply she felt as grounded and sure of herself as she ever had. She felt the light-hearted feeling in spirit Grandpa too, just before he went deep.

"In times when survival of people is a constant concern, the outside threats of starvation, shelter, and trying not to be somebody else's lunch preoccupy minds and ingenuity. Where you are today, an abundance of time and energy is spent on competing with windmills, that is to say, the existential threat of thin air, nothing but what you make up in your mind," he said.

Without saying a word, she laughed thinking to herself how at this moment she was communicating with "thin air." Grandpa answered as if she said it out loud.

"Yes I'm thin air to you, but I'm talking about a culture that competes not out of necessity, but out of ego, where there is no endgame, a waste of energy, a waste of time. People take themselves too seriously in order to achieve things that are temporary."

And the point is? She thought.

A morning breeze blew down from the hills and Bev felt a slight chill. Looking over her shoulder toward the house and along the fence line, she saw a mist rising from the grass as the sun began evaporating the water drops left overnight.

She heard her grandfather continue, "Mathias is caught in a vortex of pain and suffering that's attached to those coins gathered from the Spanish ship wreck. It was hundreds of years ago with hundreds of souls stuck in time."

I'm not stuck there, Bev thought.

"No you're not, and you have bigger fish to fry. For you, freedom from this vortex will only come by solving the mystery and recovering the treasure," he said. "Walking away at this juncture is not an option. If you try, it will haunt you and follow you."

Price and Branson? She thought.

"They could walk away and be safe, but you need them. They are not in grave danger, but you need them and they need the adventure," he said. "This is very strong energy and it won't be easy. Do not be intimidated by the challenge, however. Your capabilities are stronger than you can imagine. In the end, you can walk away from this with maturity and competence that few people have," he said. "One last thing, you will need your mother's group. They have the ability to help you overcome this vortex. There is great power there."

Bev felt a flash of fear for the first time, "What do I do with the coins?"

"When a warm breeze blows, toss them to the wind," he said.

"Grandpa, come on now!"

"Okay, okay," he said. "I get a little carried away with this whole spirit thing sometimes. Whatever you don't want, just give to somebody."

BEV WALKED through the screen porch and into the kitchen. Buzzy ran up and bounced against her leg before treating her hand to a warm cleaning. To her surprise, the boys were not standing over the map. Price was on the phone sounding like he was talking seriously to someone, and Branson sat in the corner reading the new copy of *Garden & Gun Magazine*. Bev filled her coffee cup and found a spot to sit on the back porch to call her mom. As she dialed, she noted that it was 7:30 in the morning in California.

Alice picked up on the second ring, "Well, there you are. You're quite the topic around here."

"With who?" Bev asked.

"The Group is enamored with the energy around that map," she said.

Bev took a breath to get some time to contemplate this non-news pronouncement, "Mom, do you ever get the feeling that Grandpa is still somehow around, or even talking to you?"

Alice was not expecting to hear about her dad. She picked up her cup for a sip of tea,

"Dad was a bigger than life personality. He was playful and incredibly focused when he wanted to be. Your dad and I tried to unfold every layer of his personality to get to the bottom of those complicated clues. Of all the silly games he set up for us, this was the hardest, and the one with the highest stakes. After we found the coins, I spent time unfolding the whole process in my mind," she took another sip of tea. "I felt, at the time, your grandpa was the closest person to me in the world, but at the same time I resented the trauma he put us through. I felt he had fun designing this game, but at our expense.

Holding on to that for several years, one morning a light went on in my brain, and I looked at myself, back then when it all started. I saw a meek, scared little girl, always being taken care of, always provided for and no clue who Alice Dennison really was. That scared little girl from way back then appeared like a stranger, not even a part of me now. I felt sympathy for her," Alice said.

"Wow, Mom," Bev could do nothing but listen.

"That's when it hit me like a lead-balloon. Your grandpa gave me a life...a maturity and understanding that was hard-won, but one that I needed. That was the real prize, the real payoff, not the coins."

THEN BEV HEARD Price's voice behind her, "You're not going to believe what I came across."

Bev looked up with a finger to her lips meaning she was on the phone.

"Okay," Price said and signaled to her to come in the kitchen when the call was over.

Bev turned her attention back to the phone, "Wow Mom. What a story! I never knew about all that. What happened to Dad after you found the treasure?"

"You know that part. Your Dad grew up in a way like I did. But his eyes opened to another reality. A reality that he was neither ready for intellectually or emotionally. He'd been living in a college-induced intellectual fantasy, stoked by professors who had managed to dodge the iron-grip of reality themselves, their entire lives. He saw this treasure-windfall as a clear path to entrepreneurial dominance through his natural and God-given creativity," Alice said. "New things for him like high tech, real estate, shipping, satellites...you get the picture. Small things."

"Mom, that's heavy stuff. I never heard you talk about Dad this way," Bev said.

"There aren't any secrets. I'm just spelling it out for you. Maybe it'll help you put things in perspective. Bev, your dad was settled in as a poet at 28 years old. There are many budding poets at thirteen years old. How many people do you know who are still full time poets at 28?" Alice said. "Don't bother, I know the answer. None."

Bev tried to think of a way to change the subject, because this one had left her speechless.

"Hey Mom, Branson is calling to me. I'll see what he wants and call you back," she said.

Bev slow walked back into the kitchen to see both Price and Branson standing over the map. Buzzy looked up wagging his tail.

"Oh man, wait till you hear this," Price said. "There's a cave that's well known that's just off Highway 56, about half-hour from here. Guess what it's called?"

"Buzzy's Peak," Bev replied.

"Good guess, but wrong," Price said.

"If we're playing 20-questions, just keep it coming. If not, you can just tell me the name," she said.

"Gizzard's Crawl," he said.

The words reverberated in the room and Bev heard a sort of echo. A faint light flashed which led Bev to glance at the map. The lines were slightly moving to point more north while dragging the illuminated spot with them. She looked up to see whether the boys were seeing these changes or not. Their attention stayed on Bev and not the map.

"What do you think?" Branson blurted.

All she could think to say was, "This is a hot spot. When can we leave?"

CHAPTER
TWENTY-SIX

An hour later, Buzzy jumped into the back seat of the farm truck and snuggled in close to Bev. The flashlights, snacks and one of the flood lights were in the truck bed. They pulled off Highway 70 onto route 56. There was a heavy dose of excitement in the truck cab, and no one noticed the white and brown Ford F-150, minding its own business, about a half mile back. The third dirt road from the stop sign led them through farmland of manicured pastures as well as scruffy limestone strewn woodlands.

"We should be hitting that creek crossing soon. The cave is just up the hill after that," Price said.

The creek meandered through the countryside and the winding country road mirrored its every move, but the crossing spot didn't appear.

"This is not the road," Bev said. "We need to go back and look for another turn-off."

Price looked frustrated and was not in favor of admitting defeat, but he slowed the truck and made a U-turn anyway. After all, he was not giving in to defeat, just fixing the problem.

They drove about half a mile when they passed a white and

brown farm truck nosed into the creek bed at an odd angle. All eyes were straight ahead except for Bev, who noticed an old man holding what looked like a chainsaw, walking toward the creek.

∽

THE CAVERS RETRACED their steps back to route 56, turned around and started over, driving back looking for the dirt road that had alluded them. Price slowed up when they got to the first turn. Bev looked down at the map and then up at the winding dirt road in front of her.

"No. Keep going," she said.

The same drill at the second turn, so Price slowly depressed the gas pedal and inched away. Bev looked at the map and nodded feeling sure about their direction. Suddenly she looked up and yelled out.

"Stop. It's back there," she said.

Buzzy yelped, then Branson said, "Are you sure?"

"Are you kidding? This is the blind leading the blind," she replied. Let's get this straight. I'm looking at a magic map that's lighting up with its lines moving all over the place and I'm scared out of my wits, and you want to know if I'm sure?"

Branson recoiled like a bug in a corner, "Sorry, sorry. A dumb thing to say...I wish I hadn't said it. I take it back, Sis. Your call. It's your call."

They barreled down the dirt road all eyes looking out for a creek crossing that would take them to the cave and this grand adventure. Just as they descended the backside of a small hill and disappeared from the turn, a white and brown nondescript F-150 meandered along the road heading back to route 56, looking for signs of a farm truck with three people in it.

Price drove across the creek, up the hill, and parked in a

small clearing. He gathered the gear and led the group onto a foot path for about 200 yards, until they spotted the cave entrance. Bev unrolled the map on the grass and as she did, a vibration reverberated in her ears. A faint light on the map was slowly pulsating.

"We've got something here," she said.

A ONCE POPULAR hangout for teenagers, the cave entrance was partially hidden by fledgling native foliage. Branson lifted the flood light from the truck bed and started walking on the footpath toward the cave entrance. After a few hundred feet, Price caught up with him carrying the bag of cave gear, while Bev and Buzzy took up the rear with the lunch and the map.

Branson stopped when the path dead ended at the entrance. The gap in the rock face looked wide enough to walk in with the lamp and tall enough to walk through it upright. Turning to look back down the path, he saw Buzzy, nose down, leading the way for Bev. He noticed, partially through the ground cover of leaves, what appeared to be a crinkled, dirty aluminum can with a withered "Miller" label.

"A pretty good teen hangout. Looks like nobody's been here in a while. Where did they go?" Branson said.

Price dropped his bag from his shoulder onto the ground, looked up and said, "They're all staring at their phones at Starbucks, waiting for the next Mocha Chip Frappuccino discount special," he said with a chuckle. Branson's mouth opened, poised with the utterance, *I like Mocha Chip Frappuccino*, on the tip of his tongue, but the words didn't make it past his lips. You might say he bit his tongue, in a rare instance of humility.

Bev held the map in one hand and could feel the vibration, ever so slightly. She noticed the huge wooden beam traversing the top of the entrance seemingly holding up forty-feet of red-stained rock piled above it, shading the path.

Price saw Bev staring and said, "The beam doesn't hold up all that rock. It's just there to keep any stray stones from falling on people's heads walking through."

Branson turned to look at the entrance.

Price continued, "That's about fifty-tons of sandstone and that beam is no match for that kind of weight."

"I thought these were all limestone," Bev said.

"The acidic nature of the rainfall melts the limestone and that hollows the caves out. The sandstone is not affected by this erosion, but acts like a cap on top of the caves," Price said.

Branson looked bored like he was thinking of a Frappuccino when Buzzy showed up next to him, nose to the ground and sniffing. They walked through the entrance and past wooden doors that were wedged open by silt and sand. Parts of a forged-iron latch hung on each, rusted, worn, and out of use door. The path into the cave was groomed and covered in sand untouched by the elements except for a meandering shallow trench winding its way down the middle, a remnant of a modicum of occasional rainfall seeping into this bone-dry cavern. The ceiling appeared to be lowering as they went deeper, from maybe twelve-feet to around eight. The few big boulders that remained were rolled against the cave wall. Sunlight showed the way for a couple of hundred feet but as the cavers looked ahead, they saw only black.

Each one of them held a flashlight as they inched their way forward. Suddenly Price stopped and waved his light beam in small circles on the left wall. Branson and Bev followed, lighting up a wide, forty-foot-high cavity. Pillars of stone rose from the ground, well short of the extended roofline. The painted desert landscape came to mind for Bev. She felt it was like the vast desert, Utah-landscape sprung up here in miniature from total darkness. The ceiling arched from the ground on both sides like an architect's dome.

Buzzy wasted no time investigating his private, underground Utah-like terrain. His nose was a hundred times more sensitive than people, but he still detected no musty smell. Through this main corridor a small but constant flow of air kept these rocks breathing in and out. Bev reached out to touch the formations and again felt this rough looking material to be smooth and even slick like it was poured from a pitcher.

MATHIAS SAT in the old truck and stared out the windshield. Just downstream from the crossing, where the creek bent at a right angle, he found a grove of trees to pull the truck into and partially hide. He had lost them on the dirt roads never guessing which turn they took. But finally, he took a chance and drove to an old cave that was a high school hangout in his day. As he neared the creek, he caught a glimpse of their truck and kept driving until he found a thicket to hide the F-150.

Not wanting to get too close, his plan was to cross the creek on foot and make his way closer after they entered and moved deeper into the cave. Unlike the group, Mathias knew this cave well. Okay not exactly, well. As a teen this was where the farm kids would gather on Friday nights. None of them were interested in the caves, focusing instead on beer and kissing girls. But all the same he felt familiar here.

He reached in his front-pants pocket and retrieved two gold doubloons and a silver piece of eight from Walter's box that came with the map. He rolled them around in his hand like Chinese meditation balls, never dropping a single one. Mathias was focused and driven. He was becoming a relentless predator knowing in his heart of hearts that a vast treasure would be his.

These kids were no match for him. The riches would be all his. He knew it. He felt it. All for him.

Early on, he fantasized about buying his own Caribbean Island, or a silver Bentley convertible, or first-class travel around the world, but this kind of avarice and greed had melted away in the heat and persistence of the "quest." If there is a mind-set of being "possessed," a way to forget everything but winning…a mental state of ignoring the fallout from the search, Mathias was swimming in it. People, things, places, they meant nothing to Mathias now, caught in a zone, walled off and impenetrable, lost to reason and dangerously ominous.

He inched his way down to the river, and found a crossing point that although was not shallow, had larger rocks close together that formed a make-shift bridge he could hop across. The creek bank was soft and his boots sunk in over the sole, as he pushed off toward the first oblong stone about two-feet wide. Finally on his last hop to the opposite bank, his muddy boot slid off the rock as he pushed. He lost his balance and catapulted into a spectacular bellyflop in knee-deep water. Scrambling up to the tree line, he shivered with consternation, disgust, and frustration. He looked down, took notice of this soaking, and thought, *it doesn't matter, I will get the treasure, and it will be all mine.* The frustration evaporated from his face, replaced by a menacing grin.

CHAPTER
TWENTY-SEVEN

"Is the map still vibrating or buzzing or whatever it does?" Branson said as he walked onto the screen porch, set his coffee cup on the side table, and plopped down in the white wicker chair facing the side yard.

"About the same," Bev said. "The map's not giving up. Are you? Are you running back to California to get a 'touch-base' fix?"

"It's just that we've been crawling around that cave for two days," he said. "Okay we found a few clues, so there's that. But this place is cold and dark. To be honest, I'm running out of steam. What I mean is, this mystery could go on for a long time. I have a museum to open, and all that."

"I don't think you're opening anything without a permit, Mister Battle-worn Conquistador," Bev said.

"Are you two having a sibling squabble?" Price said.

Bev looked at Price and then back at Branson, "Okay, hop on back to the coast, just leave Buzzy here, is all I ask?"

Price stood up and walked between them to interrupt the vibe and redirect the conversation.

"Let's leave in about an hour. I think today's the day we hit pay dirt...the big payoff. Come on you two, this is the score of a lifetime," Price said. "Heroes aren't born, they're made."

"Not sure this is going to make us heroes," Bev said. "Maybe filthy rich, but heroes? I seriously doubt that."

"What about Grandpa?" Branson said. "He was a hero to all those treasure hunters who heard about the game he set up for Mom and Dad to solve."

"He's my special grandpa, but all those hero worshippers have a low bar if all they wanted were some of those coins," Bev said.

"Spoken like a true rich-girl," Branson said.

"Okay, let's pack lunch and get this train moving," Price inserted.

ALICE ARRIVED EARLY at the Paranormal Center for the meeting. Traffic was light from the foothills down to Palo Alto. She bypassed the reception desk and made her way into the meeting room where she was the first to arrive. Flipping through the small collection of books that occupied the shelves against the wall, she distracted herself until others started to filter in. Alice felt confident in her clairvoyant abilities, but she was a newbie compared to many of the others. Still, for the past day she'd felt uneasy about Bev in those caves. She used her skills to look deeper into the reasons for this anxiety, but her own emotions kept her from seeing clearly when it came to Bev. Some help was need and she hoped it would be there this morning.

The group filtered in and waited for Elizabeth to join them. Upon arriving, she sat in the circle of chairs and instantly became the focal point. Always grounded and centered, she was a poster-child for detachment. Alice was well aware that there was no hiding from Elizabeth. She could read your every thought like a book, like your soul was undressed and naked.

Stay neutral, Alice said to herself over and over like a mantra. *Stay neutral.*

Meditation lasted only half an hour, but it gave Alice an opportunity to find her grounding. Keri stood in the corner of the room in her role as energy control.

Elizabeth broke the silence of mediation, "I want everyone to bring your vibration up to a shiny gold and match my energy. We have a unique opportunity to see dark, painful energy that's been harbored for centuries, molding and festering, turning into evil."

Alice shifted in her chair, and at the same time Keri waved both arms to dissipate the tension from Elizabeth's statements.

"There are hundreds of souls in this vortex, but they are in chaos and confused and wanting release. Our group here today, far exceeds their capacity," Elizabeth paused, opened her eyes and looked around the room. "Still it won't be easy. Dark energy can be powerful. Now match me on the astral plane and we will communicate with Bev Dahl. She is the focus of our efforts today." She paused. "We'll see the energy that Bev will be face-to-face with."

Alice opened her eyes and met Elizabeth's eyes staring at her. Alice knew that Elizabeth could read her feelings of relief at the help that Bev needed, but also the fear that Alice radiated at the mention of powerful, dark energy, pitch-black, cold caves and an innocent soul like Bev in a battle with evil.

CHAPTER
TWENTY-EIGHT

The cavers stood in the center of the painted-desert dome and again gazed up at the million-year-old formations their flood-light illuminated.

"We found those coins over by that tunnel, so that's where we start," Price said. "Let's split up to cover more ground. You guys continue in the tunnel. I'll walk up that ledge and see what's up top."

Bev and Branson ducked their heads to get through the five-foot high entrance with Buzzy following in close pursuit. The tunnel's ceiling grew higher to around eight feet and after a wide stretch that opened the path up, it narrowed requiring them both to turn sideways to pass through. Buzzy darted through ahead of Branson and was the first to discover a large room with columns reaching floor to ceiling.

"How many millions of years for the stalagmites and stalactites to grow and join up like this?" Branson asked.

Bev scanned the formations with her flashlight. A chill riveted her body not only at the sight of these austere rock formations, but at the chill in the air, and that total darkness that was still hard to ignore. She felt isolated and alone. Her first thought was to turn and run. Standing her ground, she took a deep breath, and as she exhaled felt a sense of comfort fill her whole body. At that moment, the fear and panic disappeared. The darkness and even the cave itself faded from her thoughts.

Her mind flashed on *bigger fish to fry,* and instantly darted to a different place, not this cave, not even this planet. She thought *I'm in a different time,* but then knew without thinking that there was no time where she was. She knew things instantly without any sense of time or place.

Then seeping into her ears, she heard the sound of wooden beams cracking, the howling of the wind, and screams, people screaming. There was no boat, no storm, no treasure, no gold or silver coins, only screaming and fear. She knew these were the same sounds from the coin in the sand at Palm Beach many months ago, but months or years or decades evaporated and the screams were all there was. Fleeting thoughts of *I should run, I should do something* flew past her and away as she stood, detached and fearless.

AT THAT VERY MOMENT IN California, Elizabeth spoke to the group quietly, "Come up to match my energy. I am with Bev on the astral plane. She's surrounded by fear, pain, and evil. No, it's not her pain, but there is danger for her. She is growing her ability very fast, but will need our help. I'm sure of it."

Alice was shaking inside and felt a bead of sweat roll down her forehead. Guilty thoughts began to riddle her mind, *I should have seen Mathias more clearly...this map thing was a tipoff...Bev reached out, but I was blind to it all. Nobody is normal who obsesses like that strange cousin of ours.*

Keri moved from beside the wall into the center of the room, stopping behind Alice to lay her hands gently on Alice's shoulders. She emitted a mild but pronounced laugh as a way to remind Alice not to take this energy she was seeing too seriously...remain objective...detached.

She leaned over and spoke into Alice's ear, "Don't own that energy. Slide it down your grounding cord and give it to the universe," she paused to let it settle in. "This is Bev's adventure, not yours. We can turn the heat down for her, but she has to fight the fire."

Bev recovered and along with Branson explored the edges of the entire cavern, looking behind rocks and crevices for hidden passages, more coins or any clue. They were also ready and willing to stumble upon any pirate treasure boxes that appeared, but like the other times, they found nothing. Finally it was time to go and Branson pointed the light toward the passageway back. Buzzy took the hint and darted off ahead of the light beam through the pitch-black tunnel. At the end, Bev and Branson stooped to get through the entrance and emerged into the big room. Their eyes adjusted slowly as they focused on a grinning Price.

"And you are so happy because of just what?" Bev said.

"Nothing. I just feel like good things are going to happen," Price said. "Oh yeah, and there's the small fact that the map is vibrating. I've heard it echoing through this cavern for ten minutes. That's got to be a good thing, right?"

Bev turned her head away and stared at the wall. She knew that comment was directed to her, but she'd been seeing that rolled up pain-in-the-butt map vibrate and move for months and never knew what to think.

"Sure. It's a great sign," she said.

She threw her head back in a dramatic gesture and said, "I'm seeing it all clearly now. Yes it's all coming to me...this is the time...the time...the time for... lunch."

She stepped forward, threw her arms out in front, and took a formal bow.

"Come on Sis. We need some meat on this bone. Let's find some treasure," Branson said.

"I'm getting some meat on my sandwich, you take care of the treasure," she said.

THERE WAS a slight shuffle from a small hidden tunnel that an ancient stream carved out and abandoned, millions of years ago. A muted echo reverberated through the chamber, and would have been heard by all, if their voices had been quiet, but the sounds were buried under the weight of their back-and-forth banter. Mathias used this time to reposition himself and stretch out slightly from the crouch he was in on the dry sand.

His mind raced with anticipation. The map was speaking and his time was near. While the cavers ate lunch, Mathias thought back and tried to make sense of the map and its changes. *Was the gold moving around, and if so, how, or who was doing it. Spirits? Okay, I'll give in to spirits, but they aren't moving any boxes of coins through a thousand miles of caves. Maybe the treasure was always here and the map was deceitful...lying about the other caves. Wait a minute what if there were other boxes, spread all over?* ...And no, no, no, he groaned. *What if there is no treasure and this is all a hoax.* And then he broke into a cold sweat. *What if the treasure was not riches, but esoteric riches like finding something deep inside yourself? A metaphor for treasure?* He shouted in his mind. *This is not a Disney movie...I'm going to find it and be rich...rich...rich, and it'll be all mine.*

Price slid off his perch on the rock and picked up his backpack, reaching in the small zippered front pouch, he broke off a piece of a power bar. Buzzy came running when Price called, and slurped up the treat. Then Price took two silver pieces of eight from the pack, put them into his hand, stooped down and opened his palm for Buzzy to sniff. As he did, Price nodded and said out loud to Buzzy, "Yes these, these coins." His nose close to the ground, Buzzy didn't look at Price. *He's after it*, Price thought.

Price couldn't control the grin on his face, so he didn't try. Bev smiled and giggled while Branson tried to remain somber, but failed and returned the smile. Bev thought, *this is not a life and death quest for these guys...but they don't know what I know and they can't fathom the dark energy I'm seeing.*

"Hey guys, grab your lights and follow me. I found something really interesting," Price said.

They walked toward a dark wall with no expectations. Price stopped, looked over his shoulder, then squeezed past a group of three stalagmites into a hidden tunnel that quickly opened into a grand passageway. They walked for a few minutes when Price stopped and said, "Look at this beauty."

It was a wooden staircase that hugged the side wall and extended vertically beyond their light beams. Branson stepped on the first step and pressed down. He mounted both feet on the step with all his weight, then he climbed to the second and third steps.

"This bad-boy is sturdy, at least down here," he said. "What's up there?" he continued as he pointed toward the top.

"That's what we are going to find out right now," Price replied.

"A box full of coins, I'm guessing," Branson said.

"You guys go find the treasure and shout down just how rich we are," Bev said.

They cautiously rose one step at a time. Bev sat and watched. There was nothing about this cavern that reminded her of treasure.

They reached the top of the stairs, stepped off onto a sand covered path and into a six-foot high tube of hollowed out limestone.

"How do these caves get here high above the main one down there?" Branson asked.

"Probably this one was here first and the water level dropped and formed the ones below," Price said. "At least that's someone's theory. Come on, let's see how far this guy goes back.

THE EXCITEMENT RAN high and time flew by for Price and Branson. Conversely, Bev sat in the dry sand and leaned against the wall. She flopped the palm of her hand on the rolled-up map without a thought. After a minute, she noticed that the map was not reacting with anything she could sense. *Either the map is taking an afternoon nap or it has no interest in this part of the tunnel.* She unrolled it and placed small rocks at each corner. She dug around in her pack and found the small black flashlight with the rubber handle, the map light. A faint glow on the spot of Gizzard's Crawl still marked their location, but no pulsating or line movement. *That doesn't really mean anything,* she said to herself, then scanned the entire map surface. *Yeah, well, yes it does. Trust yourself. You know what you know, and logic is not the main element in this puzzle. Go with your feelings...what you KNOW. The box of goodies is not going to be found here,* she concluded.

She rolled the map back up and slide the rubber bands around it. Fluffing her pack into a make-shift pillow, she stretched out and closed her eyes. She left the flashlight on lying next to the map.

She woke when the guys were backing down the ladder. Branson slipped his pack off his shoulders and let it plop to the ground creating a slight echo through the cavern. Price followed in silence.

"Okay, so what did you find up there?" Bev asked.

"Not much. Let's go. I'm tired," Price said.

Bev could see that the balloon had popped, and the hot air had pretty much seeped out, leaving the guys with burned-out enthusiasm.

∽

"So we're not rich?" Bev said when the truck was back on the dirt road and headed for home.

"Let's talk about something else," Branson said.

Price pulled into the gravel parking lot of Butcher's Stone Ground Pizza. He walked straight for the wooden table near the bar, not bothering to even glance at the high-top table in the far corner with his initials carved into the top in two places.

"Hey stranger. Haven't seen you in here for a month of Sundays," the waitress said.

"Hi Rose," Price said. "Staying busy these days. How's life treating you?"

"'Bout the same," Price's muddy boots caught her attention. "Looks like you guys' been busy. Where you been?"

"A couple of out-of-towners who wanted to see some genuine Tennessee caves," he said.

"There's plenty of places to get messy in caves around here," she said. "You can work up an appetite doing that. I'll bet you need something cold right now. Yazoo just sent over a new summer keg. Want three of those?"

"Yes, three," Bev interjected. "I don't know what the guys want."

"Ha ha," Bronson said. Looking up he said, "Just start with three. If my big sister has three beers, she'll be crawling out of here."

Rose looked over her shoulder at the bar and yelled, "Hey Bo, three Yazoo's.

She was back in a flash. She put the cold mugs in the center of the table and said, "Where'd ya'll go today?"

"That old cave everybody's been to. You know that one, Gizzard's Crawl," Price said.

"How did that go?" Rose asked.

"Okay, I guess. Same-old, same-old."

"The reason I ask is because nobody goes out there much anymore," Rose said. "One kid went a little nutty there."

"They all drink too much anyway," Price replied without much thought.

"Rumor is, he was sober-as-a-judge. A few weeks later Clyde Johnson's sister started ranting that she was going to be rich and started yelling 'all mine, all mine,' ran into the cave and nobody found her for two days."

"No way," Price exclaimed.

"Exactly. Get this. She didn't speak a word for a month. And then had no idea what happened to her."

Branson was locked on Rose listening to her story. He looked across the table at Bev. Her eyes were wide open and her pupils turned from blue to a dark, smokey-gray. The juke box blared out a country favorite flooding the empty spaces in the room. She shuddered in her seat.

On the short drive home Branson and Price talked about the

cave and strange events. It might not have risen to the level of fear, but there was a high degree of caution in the air.

BEV'S EYES opened and focused on the window curtains. The filtered light of daybreak around the edges was absent. She rolled over to look at the clock...*way too early*, she thought as she rolled over on her side to make an attempt back to sleep. Finally her sleepy eyes opened again. She looked at the clock, *Half-hour, not bad*, she said to herself as her legs quietly rolled out of the sheets, on to the floor, and transported her to the kitchen.

As much as she wanted this treasure hunt to be over, she remembered what Grandpa told her, and she still felt deep down that she wanted to be a winner. She wanted to solve this puzzle.

As contradictory as it may sound, Bev was scared to death by the strange events and the black energy that surrounded the map, but at the same time she felt confident. She felt capable enough to win and be successful.

With a big win under my belt, maybe I'll head back to California and settle down in the coastal hills, perfect weather and left-coast dreamers everywhere. She sat at the table and lifted the hot cup of green tea to her lips. *Maybe Price will come with me...or maybe I'll get some land in Tennessee and be a farm girl, and that guitar thing doesn't look too hard, after all Grandpa was a native. I've got country roots.*

Price and Branson were up earlier than Bev expected. With their high-hopes having been crushed and splattered on the ancient limestone formations, she thought they would loath opening their eyes to face the what-do-we-do-now question. In spite of all that, by eight in the morning, the farm truck rolled onto the blacktop of Highway 70 and they were headed to the cave.

MEANWHILE WHEN DAWN broke and the first light cracked through the tree line, Mathias opened the door of the old truck parked next to the stream. He knew he had several hours before he could expect company, but just to be safe, he parked downstream in his usual hiding place. He walked upstream to the car crossing and shuffled through the light flow of water toward the cave. His plan was to find a hiding place to monitor the group and be ready to react, or take charge if he needed to. First he wanted to find out what they found and where they'd been searching.

Seeing them leaving yesterday with heads low and no talking, he knew this wasn't exactly the look of finding treasure, no joy, or exuberance. More like a big dead-end. He opened his mouth and said the words in silence, *Walter tried, I have tried, maybe this is too hard.* He took a breath. *Stop! You got this. You asked for a seer and the map brought you Bev. She can read the map and she will find it for you. Watch, listen, be ready.*

Mathias spent the next couple of hours in the cave. He stumbled upon the stairs, climbing them like the guys had done, and meticulously scouring the tunnel. From the end of the passageway, he turned to go back to the top of the ladder, when a glint of light flashed in his eyes. He got down on his knees and sifted through the sand until his fingers clasped a round, flat object. Mathias knew what he had, a gold doubloon. The flashlight beam confirmed it: Emperor Phillip V, 1724, the same as the one from Walter's box.

Mathias sat back on the sand and fought off a feeling of elation, succumbing to frustration and confusion. *"Another dead-end?*" he whispered to the silent cave walls. Pulling out a garden trowel from his pack, he jabbed the point into the sand only to watch it bounce off the surface. He angled it as if uprooting a summer marigold, but the tool hit solid rock. Sweat rolled down his forehead and into his eyes blurring his vision. He dropped the trowel and slumped back.

Finally, he looked at his watch and stood up, grabbed his pack and slowly backed down the stairs to the main tunnel. He meandered back the way he came walking like a man who was broken and defeated. Then suddenly he stopped. The cave was faintly echoing a noise. He listened for half a minute and then knew. It was voices. The group was here early and he was caught. Walking cautiously, he stopped and stood at the entrance to the large cavern, about two feet back and partially hidden behind an outcropping. He was so close, but it was so black-dark he virtually disappeared.

"Hey Branson, flip the floodlight on. I want to look at the map," Bev said.

She secured the four corners before taking a bird's eye view of the whole thing. She felt the energy and could see random pulses of light flashing, but no exciting revelations or insights emerged. Bev ran her fingers along one of the lines and could see it ever-so-slightly veer to the right. Her finger followed and a warm...no, hot sensation hit her fingertip and ran up her arm, that threw her back on the sand.

"What was that?" Price said.

Shaken and disoriented, Bev said in a meek almost distant voice, "I really don't know."

But as she uttered the words, she knew the real truth. The whole picture was coming into focus, not there yet, but moving,

moving toward the finish. She reached into her side pocket and clutched the small wooden cross.

The guys started to talk back and forth. It seemed like useless chatter to her, and Bev felt like she was seeing the whole room from the top of the ceiling, detached and floating. Her attention was slowly diverted to a dark area at the other end of the room. Branson explored that corner yesterday, but didn't see any promising options. She stood and quietly walked over to the place. Stooping down and taking a few duck-walking steps, she shined the light along the floor line. *That's it*, she said to herself.

With no inflection in her voice, she said, "Hand me that miners hardhat with the light on the front."

Price stopped and looked her over with a troubled eye. There was something different about her.

"Where are you going?" Price said.

"Into that crevice. The little one over there," she said.

"You mean that slit in the rock? Branson replied. "You can't even get in there."

"You can't, but I can," she said.

"Bev, I don't know what you're thinking," Price said. "Dropping into an unknown crevice like that is crazy dangerous. If you get stuck or lost, we may never find you. Your light could go out, and three days without water...it's the end," he paused to take a breath. "Absolutely not, not going down that hole."

Bev loaded her backpack with a new water bottle, an extra flashlight and a handful of power bars. She sat in front of the crevice, shined the light into it and tossed the pack into the dark abyss.

"Bev, NO," Branson screamed.

Buzzy came alongside Bev, looked down the crevice and barked once.

"I know, I know," she said. "I've got this."

She arched her back and slid down feet first. Buzzy barked again.

Branson ran to the crevice opening, "Bev, Bev? Are you all right? All good down there?"

"A little dark," she said.

"Very funny," Branson replied.

"You guys stay tuned. I can literally smell this treasure," she said with a grin that no one saw.

CHAPTER
TWENTY-NINE

I n California, Alice's hand dropped her wooden spoon onto the stovetop. It bounced once and splattered soup broth on the burner plate. She straightened slightly and took a half step back. There was a swirling in her head and she felt a frightened pulsating feeling. Making no sense to her, she knew one thing and only one. It was Bev's fear she felt. She wanted to do something, but didn't know what. *Call Elizabeth... no. Elizabeth will already know and be looking at the energy.* Alice sat quietly to watch this unfold. *You will know when it's time,* she thought.

～

PRICE AND BRANSON WERE SPEECHLESS, aimlessly staring into the cavern. Finally Price started pacing around with no destination...just pacing. After a half-hour, he grabbed his pack and walked to the tunnel leading to the stairway from yesterday's exploration.

"Wait, I'm coming with you," Branson said.

Mathias turned sideways behind the six-foot high grouping of stalactites to divert his eyes or any inadvertent reflection from giving his presence away. Branson stopped about five feet from Mathias' hiding spot to adjust his backpack. If his light inadvertently flashed toward the wall, Mathias would be caught. He held his breath, focusing on not moving a muscle.

When the sound of their walking faded away in the distance, he carefully made his way into the cavern and headed for the cave entrance. Letting the moment settle, he wanted to see how things would unfold. He knew they couldn't leave the cave with any treasure without being seen.

He kept his light low and avoided illuminating the walls. Turning to look down he saw his old friend, the map, glowing ever-so-slightly. His fingers wrapped around the tube, lifted it up, and without any hesitation, briskly walked to the cave entrance and the mid-day sun. His eyes took a few minutes to adjust as he sat on a boulder. Relaxing his fingers, he watched the map drop to the ground. He opened his mouth drawing a few breaths of clean, country air. He could taste the sweet relief from the stale smell in the cave.

Mathias thought about the events in the cave and Bev's sudden vanishing act. Encouraged at her sudden epiphany and focus on the treasure, he had to agree with Price that sliding into that crevice alone was dangerous and fool-hearty. In his youth, he knew a boy always showing off who pulled the worst move of his short life by disappearing in a nearby cave. They found him a week later in a little-known cavern laid out like a mummy in the sand.

After a few minutes, Mathias un-scrolled the map with both hands focusing only on the illuminated section. The map was warm to the touch and the spot marked "Gizzard's" was almost bubbling off the page. He grinned as if to say, *finally...finally...I finally got this.*

Back in California, with no meeting scheduled ahead of time for the group, Elizabeth sat in the conference room, eyes closed and waiting. Keri arrived first, followed by the other member of the group, and finally Alice arrived and sat across from Elizabeth.

"Thank you for joining me with no advance notice. As you all can see, the energy is stirring and the risk for our Bev is high. I've been controlling the dark energy all morning, but things are squeezing through the cracks," Elizabeth said. "Everyone please match my energy."

Alice felt the vibration rise in the room. She was gratified, but terrified at the same time.

At that very moment, deep in the bowels of Gizzard's Crawl, Bev felt a surge of confidence offering some relief to her anxiety that was growing with every step into this unknown black hole. The walkway grew wider as she traversed, but the path was strewn with baseball-size rocks released from the ceiling. Her hands stretched out on both sides to push off the walls. Like the formations before, the rough-looking pitted stone was as smooth as marble.

Doubt and fear tried to creep into Bev's mind, but in some sort of state of bliss, she was able to shut out the outside world. She heard a flapping sound and flashed her light to the top of the cave. A bat hung upside down with its wings extended. Her eye caught more movement and the beam of light revealed not one but a group of bats. *Maybe Herman Munster lives here*, she whispered under a slight giggle.

She thought about going back, but thought, *you can't go*

back, no retracing steps, always move forward. The stark reality crossed her mind when she thought hard about retracing steps. Beads of sweat rolled from her forehead. She didn't really know where "back" was in this cave. Besides some force was pulling her forward...relentless, and not giving up...stronger and stronger with each step.

What a fine job I've done. From Wall Street to Gizzard's Crawl in Hicksville, Tennessee. Lost, cold, a crush on a boy I hardly know, and adrift in an obscure cave. Still she walked on as two hours swirled her through the hollowed-out remnants of an ancient river.

BACK IN CALIFORNIA ELIZABETH spoke to the group, "The dark energy is seeing souls abandon it, desperate to escape centuries of suffering, but it is not weakening," she said. "Imagine a clear, glass-like barrier around Bev. The energy will pass through the glass and not stick. She'll need this because the evil is getting more agitated and may strike out."

IN THE CAVE, Bev saw her narrow tunnel widen and while keeping her pace, her light scanned up to a ceiling at least forty-feet high. The walls were vertical giving the room a mass that dwarfed anything they had seen. It took her breath away. Her flashlight beam faded at that distance, only barely revealing the intricacy of the limestone formations on the far wall. *This is a castle, a grand castle,* she thought.

The small pipe-organ formations, significant in the other caverns, only complimented the massive flutes that appeared to flap open through the ceiling like giant gladiator spears composed of frozen, cotton twill, stuck in time. There were layers of dripped stone forming strata like building blocks in this fantasy castle. Where the walls narrowed, Bev followed her meager beam of light through the slim passage and found the second magnificent room. Frozen bubbles of rock seemed to cascade from the edges of the vertical walls here, forming a giant plateau appearing like petrified foam. She kept walking around this formation, shinning her light, looking. Then she rounded one outcropping which flowed to the sand floor from a terrace eight-feet above. A slight rustle in this dead-still cave caused Bev to look up to see a bat winging through the air, followed by another and another. She reached for the cross in her pocket while stopping next to a cluster of small stalactites. They were next to the base of the plateau, which grew from the sand floor one and two-feet high, pointed and sharp like spears piercing the cold cave-air.

THREE-THOUSAND MILES AWAY, Keri was the first to feel the dark energy fill the room.

"There's a panic in the energy field. This powerful entity knows we're watching. It has owned this vortex for three hundred years," she paused.

"Oh, this is really a new one for me," Elizabeth said. "This vortex has fed off hundreds of devastated souls. As they escape and gain release, the vortex is threatened.

"I am seeing that it is poised to do anything it can to survive," Keri said. "Anything to survive," she said sternly as a warning.

The group seemed to simultaneously shuffle in their chairs.

"I can see that Bev feels the attraction of the energy, but is not aware of it, or its power," Alice said. "I'm worried."

The group sat quietly as each one watched the energy in the cave. None of them had awareness of the cave itself, the darkness, or the cold, just the energy fields that were in play.

Without warning, a glass flower vase flew off the bookshelf and was hurled against the wall. Keri looked up and came out of trance to see the glass of a photo shatter in its frame. The chairs felt like they were dancing in place on top of the rumbling floor. Alice looked up terrified. Mary, the newcomer jumped up, ran to the door, and disappeared. Two of the group dropped to their knees and sought shelter under tables in the room. Elizabeth sat still, without a move, and smiled.

"Very, very powerful. I will call in Ezekiel, my spirit master," Elizabeth said.

Alice heard about Ezekiel, but also knew that he was rarely called upon. He only communicated with the most advanced mortal spirits. People without the training and depth were at risk. It was rumored that this spirit guide did not toy with mortals...he did not dance around solutions to nurture the uninformed. He always cut to the truth without regard to collateral damage. If Elizabeth is calling on him, this was real trouble. Alice was relieved and terrified all at the same time.

ALONE AND SHIVERING in the blackness, Bev looked around this space, a relic of millions of years. Panic tried to flare up in her mind, but she instantly shook it off and continued listening to the call of this unknown vortex. Turning to follow the rock wall, she caught a glimpse of something. With no urgency, she turned back, took the short few steps to an outcropped rock shelf. Her light trained on the object and she could hardly believe what she saw. A wooden box of rough-strewn planks about four-feet in length sat in the sand, alone with no disguise and no protection.

Bev studied the box carefully as she stooped down to touch the wood. *I guess it's real*, she thought. A light dusting of cave-sand slid off the surface as she tugged at the edge of one of the boards. A slight creaking sound answered her effort, but the board did not give way. She rummaged through her pack for anything that might help. Her fingers wrapped around the handle of a small garden trowel. Wedging the pointed tip between two boards, she pushed down. Another creaking sound came as the board pushed against the iron nail, but it wouldn't let go. She moved the trowel to the corner and the slight gap in the planks. Again, the pointed tip slid in and she pushed down. The wood groaned against the ancient nail, and she felt the trowel jerk as the nail let go and the board freed-up.

When she got that first board off, she looked inside, and her light illuminated two leather straps stretched over a barrel-domed box covered in what appeared to be a thin leather fabric. The next two boards were harder to dislodge, and as she pried, the trowel handle began to weaken. Finally, one of the boards released and she was able to pull it off and lay it on the sand. She reached in and flipped the clasp holding the lid on the chest, but still only allowing the lid to barely open. She propped it open with a small rock before shinning the light through the crack. The reflection through this small sliver flashed into Bev's eyes causing her to look away. She reached in her pocket and touched the cross, while holding the flashlight at an angle and looked into the box again.

Filled to the brim, the coins practically fell out of their safe abode... *a chest...THE treasure chest*, Bev thought. Her small hand slid through the opening and pulled out a handful of coins. She opened her fingers and counted eight silver disks. Eight Pieces of Eight.

MATHIAS SAT on the ground with a boulder for a backrest, rigid like a man obsessed with greed, no room in his life for boredom, melancholy, or loneliness. He slept, but only for short periods. He ate, but mostly meat and fast food. Friends? No time. Recreation? No time. The treasure must be his. Without it, his life would not be sustainable, so there was no thought of failure.

He spread the map out over the flat part of the trail leading to the cave just for one more look. After watching small movements of lines and places on the map for over a year, those things didn't surprise him. What he saw on the map today caused his eyes to bulge and fill him with excitement. Lines were actively moving on the page and the spot marked, Gizzard, was pulsating.

"This is no ordinary day," he said out loud for the warm, summer breeze to hear. "This is THE day."

Mathias lodged the map under his arm and began to trot toward the cave entrance. All the caution and clever spying that characterized the last month, vaporized into the muggy southern air. He hustled through the entrance tunnel and into the cavern where he picked up the map a short time ago. He stopped, looking around for signs of Price or Branson, ready for anything that could stand in his way...to get to HIS treasure. The echo of his footsteps faded and the room was deathly silent. Looking at the tunnel leading to the stairs, and then to the slit in the rock that Bev slipped through, he saw no movement, nothing.

He clumsily opened the map to find the next direction to

follow. Holding it up in front of him, he moved to Bev's departure spot, and then to the stairway tunnel that Price and Branson took. The closer he got to that one, the more the map reacted with vibrations and light flashes. He knew where to go. Making his way through the low, narrow first section, he picked up his pace where the tunnel widened.

CHAPTER
THIRTY

Buzzy waited on the sand as Price and Branson took another tour of the tunnel at the top of the stairs.

"I can't believe a perfect hiding place like this isn't the resting place for treasure. After all, we found some coins there. Let's take one more look," Price said.

After ten minutes, Buzzy gave a slight bark when Branson touched down from the stairs and onto the sand. Price was guarded but mostly embarrassed when he stepped down next onto the ground.

"Okay, we're going to follow the tunnel deeper and forget these blasted stairs," Price said.

Branson looked down the tunnel then took the first few steps into the dark with Buzzy in the lead. His thoughts of treasure and riches were interrupted by fear and anxiety about Bev. *Is she obsessed and being controlled by this map force or whatever it is, just like Mathias?* He thought. They walked on without conversation.

The tension built and finally Branson yelled out of frustration and fear, "We need to find Bev. I don't want to even talk about this treasure or the stupid map. Bev is my sister and we're down in the bowels of the pitch-black earth in South Po-dunk, Tennessee with no clue where she is or how to find her."

Price stopped walking and looked over at Branson. He saw a scared rich kid, accustomed to getting what he wants, when he wants it. Branson never saw a problem his mom or dad couldn't solve for him.

Then he looked at the cold hard facts. A dark, cold cave, a lost girlfriend, and a magic map that he didn't understand.

He kept silent for a few minutes and then like a pirate walking off a plank in the deep, salty sea he said with resolve and determination, "Keep going. We'll find her. Follow Buzzy."

MATHIAS DID NOT HEAR any noise in the cave as he passed by the stairs. He didn't bother to stop there. The map was leading him deeper into the dark unknown. The light pulses stayed steady and the map commanded his adherence.

"I don't need cousin Bev anymore. The map is finally showing the way to me," he whispered to himself. "Soon it will be all mine, the treasure, all mine. These little foolish children can go back to their simple, regular, boring lives."

A HALF HOUR felt like an eternity for Branson as each step was painstaking on this stretch with softball-size rocks covering the path. Buzzy circled back every little while and on one pass, Price lured him over with a piece of power bar. He pulled out the silver pieces of eight and again put them in front of Buzzy's nose. The snack disappeared quickly and Price watched Buzzy take a momentary interest in the coins. He encouraged him with the, *good-boy, good-boy, go-get-it*, command.

"Buzzy is on it. I know he is," Price said.

They continued until they saw a large opening appear that connected to their tunnel on the left side. Price stopped and shined his flashlight into this passageway, but decided to stay straight, guessing it was the best direction. After about a hundred yards that shaft narrowed to a dead-end. Retracing their steps, they tried the left turn and after a few yards, found a large opening, and a smooth sand floor with only a few obstacles. Buzzy appeared, circled them once, looked up directly at Price, barked, and took off running ahead.

When Mathias reached the left tunnel, he had no need to hesitate. The map was clear, and he obediently turned left and followed its direction.

BEV COULD HAVE GRABBED the next board to yank it loose to see the entire treasure, but she was exhausted and worn out from the stress of being lost in this dark underground tomb. Her momentum and drive vanished as she went from a crouching position to plopping on the sand in front of the chest. Taking a deep breath, her hand again found the cross in her pocket. She held it for a few quick seconds to feel the energy and the sensation of safety that was reassuring. Then next to the cross, her fingers found the doubloon in her pocket, Grandpa's gold doubloon that she aways carried for good luck, or any luck as it turned out.

She grasped the round disk while her thumb stroked the assayer's intricate work on the surface. Grandpa Richard's appearance to her often happened when she rubbed the coin. *Where are you Grandpa?* she whispered. She sat and felt like a ten-year-old version of herself...mind blank...no worries... waiting to be told the next move. This was a moment of quiet bliss for her and she had no urge to interrupt it. No gold, or silver, or map, and no cave...nothing interrupted the spell she was in.

Bev felt a relaxation of the tension in her temples moving through her shoulders and down her spine. Minutes that may have been hours passed. She was making no note of time. The chill of the cave air fell away and she felt a warm energy fill her body. A small blue dot of light appeared through her closed eyes, growing to reveal a space beyond the blue, beyond time. She settled in asking for nothing, receiving nothing, just the void.

Her mind's eye moved beyond seeing and she felt the presence of Grandpa. Another entity materialized alongside him. Unfamiliar but comforting, she greeted this apparition, Ezekiel, the spirit master.

Her months of confusion, ambition, and fear around the treasure hunt, the map, a crazy cousin, and deep cold caves were absent inside the blue light. In the blue light there were smiles, laughter, and amusement. *What about the danger? What about my need for help?'* She thought.

Chuckles and smiles reflected back to her. Grandpa and this spirit guide were not in a place of fear, rather a place beyond fear, a place of all knowing. Bev shifted her sitting position, but remained in the blue light, while sitting in the sand.

BUZZY ROUNDED the large boulder but didn't break stride, running beneath the first large domed cavern, through the passage and into the next cavern. His eyes perceived the weak glow of Bev's flashlight, but his nose led the way. He trotted past the rock shelf, the field of small stalagmites, screeching to a halt next to Bev.

She felt Buzzy's warm tongue on her hand and slowly opened her eyes. The low, cave glow from her flashlight filled her eyes, but the blue light did not disappear from her thoughts.

"Buzzy, how did you get here?" she said in a whisper.

He licked one more time then circled Bev to stand in front of the chest. His nose found the opening as he sniffed the contents of coins. There was no smile on his canine face, but Bev could feel the confidence in him that this success brought him. She sat still with no motivation to stand up or interrupt the moment.

She closed her eyes, but the blue light so prominent minutes ago was gone., and she could feel the chill from the cave seep back onto her skin...goosebumps. Suddenly Buzzy stood up and moving in front of Bev, uttered a single bark. Bev rose to her feet hearing a faint sound echo through the cavern. She waited and watched and about the time she noticed a bit of light, Buzzy took off running.

She heard Price's voice, "Look, it's Buzzy," he said.

"Hey Buzz," Branson chimed in. "Price, look at the size of this cavern. It's ten times the size of our little map-room. Buzzy is coming from that passage over there. Let's take a look at it."

Buzzy ran back to Bev.

Then Bev yelled, "Hey guys, you found me."

"You worried us to death, disappearing like that," Branson yelled out, training his light on the path ahead.

"Yeah, well things happen," she replied. "Not sure why I did that."

She saw a shadowy figure walk around the low stalagmite formation and come into view. Branson was carrying a small battery-powered lantern, silhouetting his five-foot, ten-inch frame. A small three-pointed hat with a modest peacock feather balanced on his head, along with the lace-up, knee-high boots that made him the one-and-only conquistador on the scene.

"Bev, look at me," Price insisted. "Stop doing that! I mean you can't take off like that. It's unbelievably dangerous, and it puts everybody not only upside down, but at risk too."

Price was yelling at her, being demanding, and controlling and all those bad things a girl is supposed to run from. She thought, *I like him taking control. He cares about me, and he's totally right,* she smiled. *A real man steps up when he needs to...a real man...a real man...I want a real man...Price.*

"I'm sorry and I know I owe all three of you, including Buzzy, an apology. Something came over me and as funny as it sounds, I somehow knew to follow that tunnel. Getting lost didn't cross my mind," she said.

"Well, it crossed our minds," Branson said. "Luckily, Buzzy is a star tracker."

Bev diverted her gaze over to the chest and then back at the boys.

"Did you follow me into that crevice?" she asked.

"You mean that 'death trap?'" Branson said. "No, we gave Buzzy the scent and turned him loose. He took us past the stairs and through all these crappy tunnels. A couple of turns and we showed up here," he paused. "Now we have you back and we know a wide and safe passage back to the cave entrance and the truck. Can we finally get out of here, get some beer and pizza, and forget this stupid, loser-treasure-hunt?"

Price sat on a rock during this rant from the conquistador, and let the words float in the moist air and disappear. Bev sat stoned-faced letting a few seconds pass. She walked over and causally took the lantern from Branson, and walked over in the direction of the chest.

"Take a look at this little gem," she said.

The dusty wooden box looked nondescript and unimportant, but both boys immediately grasped the relevance of this relic. Price was first to bend over and put his hand through the opening, pulling out a sample of the extravagant loot. He looked up with eyes as big as watermelons. Bev simmered with excitement; Branson shook with delight.

"No way," Branson said. "No frigin' way! Is the whole thing full of coins?"

"You mean, are the coins just covering up the gold bars?" Bev laughed.

"You know what I mean," he said.

"Little brother, we don't care what you mean," she said. "Try to stay focused, and take off that stupid hat."

"Since when is this hat stupid?" he said.

"Since the day you bought it."

Branson turned away and looked down.

"Okay you two," Price said. "We've been doing okay up to now. Let's keep it that way.

Bev smiled and gave Price a wink. Branson looked out like he was surveying the cavern, clearly irritated.

Price took a quick couple of pulls on the next board that covered the treasure. He found out that quick-work, won't work. Resting the lantern on the box, he examined the the edges of the box and discovered small rectangular nails that looked hand made from iron. They looked like they ran deep into the plank below. The stickler was, these old-style nails had no heads, no place to slide a clawhammer under to pry them out. He took the lantern and walked around the immediate periphery looking for something left over from somebody, at some time in the past that he could use to pry the board loose.

Branson stared at the box, stood quietly, before picking up the loose board from the sand. He fit it snugly under the box lid, and pushed down, but couldn't get the leverage to loosen the top. Moving the board to the edge, he pushed up and even stooped down to fit his shoulder under it and lifted up. He strained with his back and tried to straighten his knees, but the top board wouldn't budge.

Price joined in and added his shoulder to the task. On the count of three they both pushed up from the knees and as they did, they heard a high-pitched squeak. The nails pulled out ever-so-slightly. The next push produced a high whining sound and the nails let go more. Both boys grabbed the loosened plank and lifted up, causing the nails to give way, exposing the treasure chest.

They opened the ornate box and watched gold and silver coins cascade from the sides. Bev watched Price slowly walk up to the box, reach in and fill his right hand with coins. A tilt of his wrist saw the coins pour out like sand on the beach.

Price had gone along with this treasure hunt as an adventure and because Bev had a passion for it. She knew he didn't understand the seriousness of it all, or the impact of a treasure this size. She saw the wheels turning in his head and the tertiary discovery of all the possibilities riches can bring. He did not contemplate the pain of divorce, or the pressure of opportunities that almost certainly alter a personality. She glanced over at Branson. *For example*, she thought.

When the world finds out even a hint of this windfall, nobody is your friend, because everybody is. Every compliment, every door that opens up is contrived and can't be trusted, even the genuine ones.

Bev closed her eyes and saw the small blue light as just a speck, but then open and begin to grow. The warmth, the safety, the protection of the spiritual blue light engulfed her body. She sat in that place of no time, no space and could feel the presence of Grandpa, and his smile. She thought about, *bigger fish to fry*, and smiled. In this space there were no fish, and yet there were all the fish in the world at the same time. Grandpa's smile glowed, and Bev finally understood the culmination of her quest. It was to find the truth. *All the fish and no fish at all*, she thought. *The Truth.*

What seemed like hours to Bev were only minutes to Price and Branson, who were dumping the contents of their packs onto the sand.

"Let's load up all we can carry and then come back with frame packs to get the rest," Branson said.

"If you take that tunnel I came through, we'll be doing this for a week," Bev said.

"No, Sis. Buzzy found a nice wide channel that we can stand up straight in the whole way," Branson said. "Hey Price, do you think we could roll it out in a cart? I mean push some of that debris out of the way?"

"It'd be a lot easier, but there were a couple of rough spots around that last bend in the tunnel," Price said. "Maybe we should take a look and get a feel for it. Heck, if we could roll the whole thing out, that would make it easy street."

Branson took a step toward the tunnel, turned and looked back at Bev, "Do you want to go?"

"I'll wait here," she said. "You guys do your thing."

CHAPTER
THIRTY-ONE

The cave was like a premium sound system. Everything said at one end echoed and reverberated throughout the cavern. Mathias sat behind a rock just off the path. He couldn't see the box, but he heard it all. The map laid on the sand beside him. His hand dropped alongside it, then brushed it away, a relic he had no need for anymore. *His treasure* lay in wait. His plan was formulating to let them pack out a measly amount of the coins. He would then move the entire box of coins to a new hiding place, one they would never find. When they gave up, he'd take it out at his leisure. Of course, he'd have to get that dog out of the picture. His nose was too good and Mathias couldn't risk it. Buzzy knew him from the hospital and would likely come to him for a treat. He'd be able to grab and cage him. If he started howling, he'd shoot him. No problem.

Buzzy took off down the path, but while heading for the entrance and out of sight from the cavers, he veered left with his tail wagging. Mathias flinched when Buzzy's cold nose touched his hand. He pulled back in surprise sitting stiff and rigid like a man in fear. The worst thing would be if the dog barked to get his attention, so out of desperation, he acknowledged him with a quick pat on the head, but then looked away showing no encouragement.

Mathias dodged the bullet, as Buzzy took off to lead the guys out of the cavern and away from *his treasure*. He took a chance and peered out from his hiding place. He saw Bev alone and sifting through the coins haplessly. At his feet the map lit up and vibrated, but Mathias didn't care about the map. His eyes were fixed on the answer to his quest, his dream. But like an invisible mist, the dark energy oozed from the map and surrounded the one person who would do it's bidding, grasp the treasure and return it to the sea, locking in the tortured souls to keep them trapped. Mathias didn't know it but his quest for riches would be short-lived if the map has its way.

THE PLAN, the logic, the months of caution, and cunning strategy vanished as Mathias stepped onto the path walking toward Bev. Like a ghost, he moved closer and closer making no sound. Finally Bev looked up. Startled and shocked, she made no attempt at cordial greetings. She read Mathias like an open book, and it wasn't pretty. Instinctively, her hand thrust into her pocket and clutched the cross, the cross from Walter's house that belongs to the map. The scene in front of her blurred, but all the same she perceived Mathias going into a kind of slow motion. She shimmied up the plateau of frozen limestone flows that cascaded from the vertical walls, more than two million years ago. Angled but flat enough to stand straight, the narrow flutes offered some traction as she scurried higher.

He appeared stiff and his limbs and whole body seemed constricted, trying to follow her up the plateau. Her hand emerged from her pocket with the cross. Her fingers closed tighter around it as she felt its power. She took another step higher, but when her weight shifted a few loose pebbles threw her off balance. Catching herself, she stayed upright, but her hand loosened enough to let the cross slip away. It hit the top of the rock then bounced top-over-bottom, tumbling to the sand below.

Mathias's eyes brightened. He looked around the cave and then up at Bev, and smiled.

THE FIRST FLOOR of the Paranormal Institute buzzed with classes in meditation, and clairvoyance. On the second floor in the small library, Elizabeth sat with the group. To her right sat Keri and as usual across from Alice. Elizabeth felt the shift in Bev's energy, and also the cold fear on her sweat-soaked skin.

The collective energy in the group merged into one entity, and together they called in Ezekiel. Not a thing changed in the room. The chairs stayed still. The fresh-cut flower arrangement radiated warmth. But everything changed for the group. First, a white wave of energy blanketed their consciousness, squeezing out everything else. Alice opened her eyes and felt a shock, as she noticed the cleansing of the room. A quick wave of black followed, striking fear and trepidation throughout. Next the yellow wave felt like a quick bolt of electricity, followed by green lifting the room to a higher plain. Finally, the gold wave rumbled in with Ezekiel in the center.

Everything that was important a minute ago melted away. There was no place and no time, just the gold light. Fear, anxiety, happiness, expectation, future and past melted away. With a wave of his hand, Ezekiel motioned in the direction of the lost souls whose pain and terror dominated the dark energy surrounding Bev and the magic map. All the souls looked out as if behind a bubble of glass. Ezekiel waved again and the dark energy drained out and evaporated into the atmosphere. A blanket of gold filled in and covered the space occupied by these tortured souls.

At this same time in the cave, Mathias inched closer to Bev who had exhausted her escape options and was squeezed against the vertical cave wall. The look of terror in his eyes gave Bev little hope for a good outcome. She pulled her elbow in tight to her body denying Mathias his first attempt at grabbing her. He reached out again wrapping his fingers around her wrist.

She screamed at the top of lungs, "You can have it. I don't want any of those coins."

But Mathias heard nothing but the rumble of the dark energy screaming in his ears, *take the coins, take the coins*.

BACK IN THE second-floor library in California, Ezekiel raised his hand and waved with a slight, muted motion.

BEV TRIED to loosen Mathias's hold on her wrist, but it was too tight. Then she felt a cool breeze rolling through the cavern and looked out to see a silent, black wave floating through the air. The wide-wing formation narrowed into a pointed arrow as it approached. She felt overwhelmed and closed her eyes with a resolution that she had no control of anything at this point. The formation of bats flew within inches of Bev as the first ones surrounded Mathias circling from his head to his feet. His hand fell away from Bev's wrist as wave after wave of bats covered him. He staggered a few steps away, while Bev stabilized her footing. From where she stood Mathias looked like a mummy wrapped in black.

Then she saw his balance waver as one foot stepped on a few loose marble-size stones. His hands flew out from his sides for balance, to no avail, and both feet slipped out from under him. The first bounce on the rock surface threw him into a cartwheel. Bev saw the bats swarm to the top of the cavern and circle silently as Mathias bounced off the smooth limestone surfaces and crumbled onto the floor below.

In spite of the threat that Mathias posed, Bev scaled down the rock ledge to where he laid on his back. She expected broken bones and probably a concussion. But kneeling down next to him, she saw a trail of blood running across his shirt, and then the shocking reality. The pointed end of a stalagmite pierced through the front of his shirt from behind his ribcage.

His bloodshot eyes opened and before Bev could say a word, he uttered, "It's mine, all mine."

Even this near incoherent, hostile gasp could not hold back the tears pouring from Bev's wide-open eyes as she watched Mathias struggle for his last breath.

Ezekiel again raised his hand, this time above his head, and made a sweeping circular motion. The bubble that partitioned the souls trapped for hundreds of years vaporized into thin air. Alice saw the entities escape from everywhere, the chest, from the rocks, from the sand, from all directions, and disappear one at a time until none remained.

Back in the cave, the map laid on the sand behind the rock where Mathias had pushed it away. Lost and abandoned, the map rolled slightly, emitting a faint pulse of light, then unceremoniously disintegrated slowly into a cold pile of ashes. Simultaneously and unaware of the map's demise, Alice sat back in her chair and felt a quiet resolution. *It's done.*

BEV WALKED over to the box of coins, picked up a silver piece of eight, and rubbed her fingers over the surface.

That was some kettle of fish I had to fry, Grandpa, she thought, while tossing the coin back in the box.

THE END

PREVIEW CHAPTER
HERE IS AN INTRODUCTION TO THIS SAILING ADVENTURE IN THE VIRGIN ISLANDS

Spanish Pieces of Eight
Book 1 of *Pieces of Eight* Series

Prologue

"All those gold and silver coins would be in a bank safe deposit box if Richard hadn't died Friday morning. He finally agreed to abandon this treasure hunt trick and dig up his sunken fortune. When I reached the hospice at noon Friday with the trust amendment for his signature, they were wheeling him out under a sheet." Bill Price paused, pulling the phone receiver slightly away from his ear.

A voice crackled through his phone as he pressed it again to his ear. "We know it's buried on that postage-size island in the Caribbean, let's just go get it."

"Impossible. The trust is iron-clad. All the coins stay, and the treasure hunt begins."

"We've talked about this," the voice responded. "When we buried it, silver was thirty dollars an ounce and gold was three hundred dollars an ounce. Now silver is three hundred and gold is two thousand."

"I know full well its value is around five and a half million," Bill Price said.

"Richard didn't tell you?"

"Tell me what?"

"Bruce added to it over twenty years just to humor Richard, but mostly they undercounted it on purpose. It's at least a hundred million now."

BOOK CLUB GUIDE & QUESTIONS

1. Did you feel sympathy or more of "I told you so" when Bev suddenly lost a million dollars in the first chapter?

2. Were you surprised when Bev had the catastrophic, other-worldly vision on the sand in Palm Beach? Do you think that experience intimidated her or made her stronger and more resilient?

3. Bev could have had an easy life back home. If you had the same choices of a dicey and risky adventure, or a cushy life in California, would you have chosen the same way as Bev?

4. Bev graduated in economics, considered a "hard" major, and moved to Wall Street. Knowing what you know about her now, were you surprised when her career melted down?

5. When the magic map was given to Mathias, did it feel like a dirty trick, or was it just a fluky event that went sour?

6. Did you think that Branson was dressing like a Conquistador strictly for attention, or did he have more serious personality issues?

7. Bev's mother, Alice, had experience with paranormal phenomenon, yet she cautiously trickled the information to

Bev. Should she have guided Bev more in the beginning so she could have dealt more confidently with the spirits?

8. Was Price too complacent and easy going, or should he have taken charge more?

9. Would you have questioned what to do with this found treasure, or would you have had a plan to hold on to it?

10. Did Branson get too much sympathy from his family, and was he tolerated to the extent that gave him a measure of encouragement to act eccentric?

11. Was the intervention of the paranormal psychics in California really needed for Bev to navigate her adventure, or could she have done it on her own or with the help of Price and Branson?

12. Do you think Grandpa Richard should have been able to help Bev more from his place in the spirit world? Or, was he letting her navigate this adventure on her own so she could find out more about herself?

About the Author

Rick Glaze published the kayaking adventure, *The Purple River* in 2021, *Spanish Pieces of Eight*, a sailing adventure/mystery in 2022, *Jackass a Short Story Collection* in 2022, and *Ralph & Murray* in 2024. Rick was a financial columnist in Silicon Valley for San Francisco's *Nob Hill Gazette* and the *Los Altos Town Crier*. He attended the Stanford University Creative Writing Program, and is a graduate of Peabody College, Vanderbilt University. An award-winning songwriter, with a Pandora station and Spotify Playlist, credits on Country Music Television (CMT), and BBC Radio, Rick has rafted the Grand Canyon, the Salmon and Rogue Rivers as well as sailed throughout the Caribbean Sea, and even wandered around in deep, dark caves in the Southern U.S. for the current novel.

Acknowledgments

Thanks to Cumberland Caverns in Tennessee for the introduction to the deep and very dark cave system along with Mammoth Cave tours in Kentucky. As before, thanks to the Mel Fisher Museum in Key West for the continuous education into the sunken treasure. Gratitude goes to Dr. John Keyser for his personal impressions of caving as well as the background material.

A shoutout to the San Jose Psychic Institute and the Berkeley Psychic Institute for helpful insight and helping make Ezekiel come alive for readers.

And finally, thanks to my editors and beta readers because you can't catch every typo by yourself.

www.ingramcontent.com/pod-product-compliance
Lightning Source LLC
Jackson TN
JSHW080024190225
79074JS00001B/37